Barney moved before Estomago could restrain him. With one leap, he hurled himself toward De Culo and placed an expert kick at his head. But the president ducked in time and took the blow in the meaty part of his back. Still, it staggered him and he reeled crazily into the corner of the room. Barney didn't have another chance. Estomago's magnum was drawn and lodged inside his mouth before he could rise from the spot on the floor where he had fallen.

"Take the American scum away," De Culo said, doubled over from the pain in his back. Estomago yanked Barney to his feet.

"Wait," De Culo shouted as the two men reached the door. "There is one more thing I wish to give our guest. A welcoming gift." His eyes vicious, he stumbled over to the desk and threw open a drawer. "I was saving this for later, but I think that now would be perfectly appropriate."

He reached deep into the drawer and pulled out something soft and ashen. He tossed toward Barney. It hit him on the cheek, feeling like a cold leather bag, then dropped to the floor.

And there, at his feet, rested Denise's severed hand, its thin gold wedding band still encircling the third finger.

"Your wife wouldn't take the ring off," De Culo spat. "So we took it off for her. Get him out of my sight."

Dazed, Barney allowed himself to be dragged out of the room where De Culo's laughter grew louder and louder, where the little hand with its cheap ring lay on the floor.

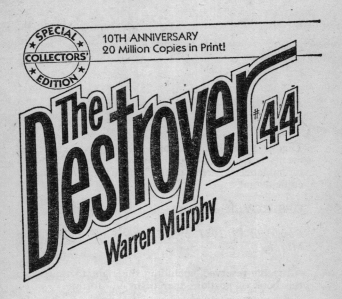

SPECIAL COLLECTORS' EDITION

10TH ANNIVERSARY
20 Million Copies in Print!

# The Destroyer #44

## Warren Murphy

PINNACLE BOOKS      NEW YORK

For Molly Cochran
and the House of Sinanju,
P.O. Box 1454, Secaucus, N.J. 07094

DESTROYER #44: BALANCE OF POWER

*Copyright © 1981 by Richard Sapir and Warren Murphy*

An original Pinnacle Books edition, published for the first time anywhere.

First printing, June 1981

ISBN: 0-523-40718-1

Cover illustration by Hector Garrido

*Printed in the United States of America*

PINNACLE BOOKS, INC.
1430 Broadway
New York, New York 10018

# FORWARD

Warren Murphy lives in New Jersey. He has been a newspaperman, a sequin polisher and a political consultant. His hobbies are mathematics, chess, martial arts, opera, politics, gambling, and sloth. Occasionally married, he is the father of four children.

He tells how the Destroyer series got started:

"The first Destroyer was written in my attic in 1963. It finally got published in 1971 and was an overnight success. In those days, Dick Sapir was my co-author and partner. He retired from the Destroyers a couple of years ago and took his name off the books when he decided he didn't want anybody to know he knew me. I helped him make this decision by locking him in my cellar for eight days without water.

"Nevertheless, he still hangs around. Various characters that appear in these pages are Dick's. Occasionally, he writes sections when someone or something annoys him. Anyone who knows him knows that this guarantees a certain frequency of appearance.

"Dick used to write the first half of books and I would write the second half. When he was mad at me, he would just send me 95 pages without a clue on how the book might be resolved. He would never write more than 95 pages. He stopped at the bottom of page 95 no matter what. Once, he stopped in the middle of a hyphenated word.

"We used to get a lot of letters and answer them, but then Dick took over answering them and lost all the letters and forgot to pay the rent on our post office box. He said he was sorry.

"In answer to the questions we get asked most: there really is a Sinanju in North Korea, but I wouldn't want to live there. There really isn't a Remo and Chiun, but there ought to be. Loud radios are the most important problem facing America. The Destroyer is soon to be a major motion picture. We will keep writing them forever."

# AFTERWORD

What have they done to Richard Sapir? And why is only Warren Murphy's picture on the cover? These and other vital questions are casting gloom over the tenth anniversary of the *Destroyer*.

By Richard Sapir

Why am I asking these questions? Because none of you did. For a year now, my byline has failed to appear on *Destroyer*, on the more than 20 million copies sold. These mind-wrenching questions have crossed exactly one other mind besides mine. And I say to the fine, sweet, noble lady: "Thank you, Mom."

The tragic fact is none of you have missed me. Sales have increased. Readership has jumped. Complimentary letters abound.

Warren Murphy, whose name now appears alone, has not even gotten a phone call in the middle of the night, perhaps saying: "You scum bag. Where's Dick Sapir? You're nothing without him."

Warren claims his phone is as quiet as a midnight kiss over a baby's crib. I know this is not so, but professional ethics forbid me from revealing my source. Just for your information, however, let it be known that he gulped and was stuck for an answer and wanted to know who the caller was.

Well, Warren, I will tell you who it was. It was your conscience.

Enough of that. I am not a bellyacher. But where

were your letters to me? Where was the begging I so richly deserved? Is a simple grovel too much to ask?

Did one of you possibly consider that you had done something wrong? Did you think you were the cause of my leaving?

Where was a simple act of contrition? All I got was a wedding invitation from an old friend now living in Colorado . . . and that was three months late and said nothing about my leaving the series. Just had some printed nonsense about his daughter getting married.

So I am gone.

And you don't care.

Well, I don't care that you don't care. In fact, I never cared that you didn't care. I was just somewhat taken aback by the depths of your not caring, its broad base and cross-community penetration.

But why should I be surprised at this time?

In the ten years that my name appeared on the series, did one of you ever dedicate your lives to me? Where were the hallelujahs? What about a Richard Sapir festival? I would have settled for nude photos and obscene propositions.

But getting back to the so-called joyous tenth anniversary—I am above it all. And I'll tell you something else. I may come back for a book or two with or without your outcry. And I still contribute significantly, and if it weren't for my father's patience, the series never would have been bought, and I buy all the typewriter paper, and Warren's typewriter has a missing key, and he can't quit smoking and I have.

And I know he went out with Geri a few years ago, and I don't believe nothing happened.

—*Richard Sapir*

For the special anniversary issue which didn't carry his picture or anything nice about him.

viii

# PUERTA DEL REY, HISPANIA
## (Associated Press International)

A man claiming to be an agent of the United States CIA held an antic press conference here yesterday and said the CIA was working on an overthrow of the Hispanian regime.

The man, who was taken into custody minutes later, was identified by General Robar Estomago, head of the Hispanian National Security Council, as Bernard C. Daniels, an escaped mental patient. He had no connection with the CIA, Estomago reported. This was confirmed by the U.S. State Department.

During his rambling, incoherent press conference, the man identified as Daniels, who was obviously intoxicated, claimed he had been a CIA agent for 15 years, the last three in Hispania.

Prior to that, he had worked in China, Japan and behind the Iron Curtain and in his travels had participated in the assassination of 74 men, he said.

Daniels accused the CIA of torturing and beating him repeatedly during a recent incarceration on the island dictatorship, and showed newsmen a grotesque scar forming the letters "CIA" on his abdomen.

According to Estomago, Daniels's wounds were self-inflicted, and resulted in Daniels's commitment to the mental institution.

Early reports from the American Embassy indicate that Daniels will be returned to the U.S. for medical treatment.

# CHAPTER ONE

It was a white neighborhood with clean, tree-lined streets and mowed lawns, free of garbage and noise and scrambling bodies. Halfway down Ophelia Street, a three-story wooden house winked through drawn blinds across the silent Hudson to New York City, squatting like a giant, crouching gray animal.

It was a nice house in a nice place, a place where a man would want to live. That is, if there were anything to live for in that house, such as a drop of tequila. Or even bourbon. Gin, in a pinch. Anything.

But for seventy-five thousand dollars, a man had a right to sleep peacefully through the night in his own house, without being shattered into consciousness by a doorbell so diabolically designed as to sound like the squawks of a thousand migrating ducks.

He refused to open his eyes. If he should catch a glimmer of light, it would destroy his sleep and then the squawking would never go away and then he would be awake.

A man had a right to sleep if he paid for his own home. He covered an ear with a palm and curled his legs up toward his chin, hoping that assuming the

3

fetal position would catapult him back to the womb, where there were no ducks.

It didn't. The doorbell continued ringing.

Bernard C. Daniels opened his eyes, brushed some of the dust from his white summer tuxedo and contemplated swallowing. The taste in his mouth told him it was a bad idea.

He pushed himself off the wooden floor that had once seen many coats of polish, but was now covered thickly from wall to wall with a gray film of dust. Only his resting place and last night's footprints broke the film. It was a barren room with a high white ceiling and old unused gas vents for lighting the house during a past era. It was his room, in the United States of America, where there were laws, in the town of Weehawken, New Jersey, where he was born and where no one crept up on you in the middle of the night with a machete. It was a place where you could close your eyes.

He was fifty years old and closing his eyes was a luxury.

His first night of luxury in many years shattered by a doorbell. He would have to get it disconnected.

Daniels stumbled to the window and tried to open it. Age had sealed it more securely than any latch.

He needed a drink. Where was the bottle?

He traced last night's steps from the door to his resting place to the window. No bottle.

Where was it? He couldn't have put it in the large closet at the other end of the room. There was no arcing sweep in the dust on the floor at the base of the closet doors. Where the hell was it?

Squawk. Squawk. Squawk. The bell sounded again. Daniels muttered a curse and broke a pane in the window with the empty bottle he had in his pocket.

4

So that's where it was. He smiled. A cool April breeze off the Hudson River flowed through the broken window. Daniels filled his lungs with the cool, fresh air, then gagged and sputtered. He would have to tape over the window, he said to himself, coughing. Too much air, and a man could breathe himself to death. He'd been so much more comfortable breathing the homey dust of the floor.

A sharp voice came from beneath the window. "Daniels!" the voice yelled. "Daniels, is that you?"

"No," Daniels quavered back, his voice hurdling over a lake of rancid phlegm. At first he hadn't known whether to answer in Spanish or English. Fortunately, he realized, "no" was the same in both languages.

The bottle was wet in his perspiring hands. He glanced at the label. Jose Macho's Four Star Tequila. He could get a gallon for a buck in Mexico City. It had cost him nine dollars at a Weehawken bar.

Squawk. Squawk. Squawk.

"Damn it," Daniels hollered through the shattered pane. "Will you stop that goddamn ringing!"

"I did," came the voice. It was familiar. Coldly, efficiently, disgustingly familiar.

*"No estoy aqui,"* Daniels answered.

"What do you mean you're not home? What other idiot would smash a window instead of answering a doorbell?"

Succumbing to logic, Daniels dropped the bottle on the floor and left the room, the squawks still sounding in his ears. He descended the wooden stairs, slowly pausing to examine all three dusty barren floors.

He walked with grace, each step the product of years of gymnastics, built into a solid muscular body

5

that 35 years of frequent abuse had not managed to debilitate. Daniels was a handsome man. He knew this because women told him so. His rugged face was topped by a shock of short, steel-gray wavy hair. His nose had been broken six times, and the last fracture restored the dignity that the first five had taken away.

A cruel face, women called it. Sometimes the perceptive ones added, "But it fits you, you bastard."

Barney would have smiled remembering that, if he hadn't been seeking desperately to burn out the barnyard-flavored coating of his tongue with a blast of alcohol. Any decent rotgut would do. But there was nothing.

Squawk. Squawk. He waved his arm in the oak-paneled foyer as though the man behind the stained glass window could see his movements and would stop ringing. No good. He fumbled with the three brass locks on the door, finally twisting the last into position.

Then, firmly grasping the tarnished doorknob as if it would fall to the floor if he let go, he pulled back hard and a gust of April swatted his face. "Ooh," Barney gasped.

A man in a stylish Ivy League blue worsted suit stood in the doorway. He wore an immaculate white shirt and a striped tie, knotted tightly, and carried a black attaché case. He had the kind of well-bred, old-money face that was accepted everywhere and forgotten immediately. Barney would have forgotten it too, except that he'd seen its smug, vain, monotonously snotty expression too many times.

"Quit ringing the frigging doorbell," Daniels demanded, refusing to let the wind blow him to the floor and amazed, as ever, that its force failed to muss the man's careful Christopher Lee hairdo.

6

"My hands are at my sides," the man said without humor.

Daniels stared into the wind. They were.

Squawk. Squawk.

He needed a drink.

"You wouldn't happen to have a drink on you, would you, Max?"

"No," said Max Snodgrass emphatically. "May I come in?"

"No," said Barney Daniels just as emphatically and slammed the door in Max Snodgrass's face. Then, watching the dark shadow on the other side of the stained glass, he waited for the outrage.

"Open this door, Daniels. I have your first pension check. If you don't open up you won't get your check."

Barney shrugged and tilted his head back, looking at the solid beamed ceilings fifteen feet high. They didn't build them like that any more. It was a fine buy.

"Open up now or I'm leaving."

And the paneling, thick oak. Who paneled with oak nowadays?

"I'm leaving."

Barney waved goodbye. And the ceiling joints.

"I'm serious. I'm leaving."

Daniels opened the door again. "Don't leave," he said softly. "I need your help."

Max Snodgrass stepped back slightly, a wary half step. "Yes?"

"An old woman is dying upstairs."

"I'll call a doctor."

Daniels raised a shaking hand. "No. No. It's too late for that."

"How do you know? You're not a doctor."

"I've seen enough death to know, Max," he intoned somberly. "I smell death."

Daniels could see the pink neck stretching, the flat gray eyes trying to peer into the house. "And you want me to do something for her, is that right?"

Daniels nodded.

"And I'm the only man in the world who can help, is that right? And it's not a loan of a few dollars because I have the check with me, right? Then it must be something else. Could it be she wants one last glass of tequila for her dry old throat before she passes on to that great desert up yonder?"

Snodgrass smiled, an evil, vicious, untrusting smile. The smile of a man who would not give a dying grandmother a drink.

"You have no heart," Daniels said. "From a man who has no heart, I will not accept the check."

"You're not doing me any favors."

"Yes I am, buddy. If I don't take the check, your bookkeeping will get all fouled up." He grinned wickedly. "And we both know what your boss will think about that."

Your boss. Not ours. Thank God.

"Ridiculous," Snodgrass said in a casual voice that suddenly squeaked. "Just add another memo to the files."

"But the CIA doesn't cotton to memos," Daniels taunted.

The pink neck grew red and the gray eyes above it flashed. "Quiet," Snodgrass hissed. "Will you shut up?"

"I'll say it louder," Daniels said. "Louder and louder. CIA. CIA. CIA."

Snodgrass glanced quickly and desperately to both sides. He slapped the oak panel of the door with the flat of his hand. "All right, all right, all right. Will you shut up? Shhhh."

"Mickey's Pub will sell it to you, and it's only three blocks away. The liquor store's six and a half blocks," Daniels said helpfully.

"I'm sure you've counted the steps," Snodgrass sneered as he turned to go.

"Don't forget to bring two glasses and a lemon."

"First take the check."

"No."

"All right. I'll be back. And shut up." Snodgrass pranced neatly down the steps to the cracked path that led to his well-polished Ford.

Squawk. Squawk. Squawk. The ducks started flying through his head again. Damn it, when would Snodgrass get back?

Snodgrass didn't knock. He walked through the open door to the kitchen where Daniels sat on the sink desperately desiring a cigarette.

"Got a smoke?"

"One thing at a time," Snodgrass said, opening his attaché case and extracting the tequila bottle.

He offered the bottle as if throwing out a challenge. Daniels accepted it as if accepting a gift from the altar of grace.

"No glasses?" Daniels asked.

"No."

"How can you expect a man to drink in his own private home straight from the bottle?" Daniels asked, twisting off the cap and dropping it into the white porcelain sink. "What are you, Snodgrass? Some kind of animal that never lived in a house? Where were you brought up, some South American jungle or something?"

Indignantly, Barney Daniels raised the bottle to his lips and let the clear, fiery liquid pour into his

9

mouth and singe it clean. He swished the tequila in his mouth, careful that it washed over each tooth and numbed the gums. Then he spat it over his right arm, twisting around so the spray splattered the sink. He softly exhaled, then inhaled. It was good tequila. Magnificent.

Finally, he took a long swig and sucked it into his whole body. The ducks disappeared.

"Cigarette," he said weakly and took another sip from the bottle.

Snodgrass flashed open a gold cigarette case filled with blue-ringed smokes. With deft hands, Daniels plucked out all of them, leaving the case shining and empty before Snodgrass could close it. He stuffed one in his mouth and the rest in his pocket.

"Those are imported Turkish, my special blend," Snodgrass whined.

Daniels shrugged. "Got a light?"

"I'd like some of them returned."

"I'll give you two. Got a light?"

"You'll return the rest."

"All right. Four."

"All of them."

"They're crushed. You wouldn't want crushed cigarettes, would you?"

Snodgrass snapped the case shut and returned it to his vest pocket. "You're a disgrace. No wonder upstairs is so happy to get rid of you."

He did not look at Daniels when he said it, but busied himself taking three form papers and a small green check from his case. "Sign these and this is your check."

"I don't have a pen."

"Return this one," Snodgrass said, offering a gold pen.

10

Daniels grasped the pen between right thumb and forefinger, looking at it quizzically. "It's not one of your idiot gas gun devices, is it?"

"No, it's not. That was always the trouble with you, Daniels. You were never a team player. You never learned to adjust to modern methods."

Daniels steadied the bottle between his knees and signed the papers in long even grade-school penmanship strokes. He finished with a flourish. "What did I sign?"

"That you resign officially from Calchex Industries for which you have worked for twenty years, the only firm for which you have worked."

"All three of them say that?"

"No. The others say that you resigned from the firm because you embezzled money from it."

"Pretty nice. Anytime I open my mouth, you can get a warrant, pick me up nice and legal and no one will ever see me again."

"Well, if you want to be crude about it, yes," Snodgrass said, his eyebrows arching disdainfully. "Ordinarily, of course, such a thing would never happen. But you're not an ordinary case." He forced the papers into his attaché case, then, smiling as though someone had just forced gravel into his gums, he surrendered the check.

"This should bring you up to date," Snodgrass said. "Your next pension check will arrive about May first." He looked Daniels up and down as though Barney were a malignant tumor. "This is just my personal opinion, Daniels," Snodgrass added, "but, frankly, it makes me sick to see you collect a pension at all, after what you did to the company back there in Hispania."

"I know how you feel, Max," Barney said sympathetically. "The company gave me the fantastic op-

11

portunity of being tortured limb by limb for three months, having my fingers broken at the hands of your local thugs, getting drugs poured down my throat, not to mention the exquisite pleasure of feeling your emblem burned into my belly with hot irons, and I have the nerve to accept a four hundred dollar check from you." He shook his head. "Some people just got no gratitude." He drank deeply from his bottle.

"You know we didn't do that," Snodgrass snapped.

"Stuff it, Max." He drank again. The liquor felt like a friend. "I don't care. You and the rest of your clowns can do whatever you want. I'm out."

"The company didn't do it," Max said stubbornly. Barney waved him away.

"Tell me something, Snodgrass. I've always wondered. Is there really a Calchex Industries?"

"Certainly," Snodgrass said, glad to be off the subject.

"What does it do besides provide pensions for cashiered CIA agents?"

"Oh, we operate a very thriving business. At our main plant in Des Moines, we manufacture toy automobiles aimed at the overseas market. We sell these to a major company in Dusseldorf. There they are all melted down and the steel is sold back to us to make more toys. All very up and up. We own both Calchex and the German company. Calchex hasn't missed a dividend in fifteen years."

"Good old American enterprise."

"Are you planning to work, Daniels?"

"Yes, yes. Quit peeing your pants about what I'm going to do with the rest of my life. I am planning on devoting the major portion of it to research on the lifesaving properties of tequila."

12

"I mean a job. We can't have you running around getting involved in wild schemes." He looked worried.

"I've got a job," Daniels lied.

"Nothing in South America, of course."

Daniels sipped some more tequila and nodded slowly. "I know what I'm allowed to do."

"Just so you know. Nothing controversial and nothing outside the borders of the United States."

"Don't worry about it. I'm going to be a librarian."

"I suppose you expect me to believe that."

"I do."

Snodgrass turned crisply to go. Before he reached the kitchen doorway, he turned back to face Daniels. "I'm sorry things didn't work out for you," he said, suddenly contrite about his crack that Barney didn't deserve his paltry pension. Daniels had been one of the best agents the company had ever used. And use him it had, over and over, in missions where none of the CIA's expensive gadgetry was worth a fart in the wind next to Barney's courage and cunning.

There had been no one better. And now there was no one worse. Snodgrass looked to Daniels, sucking on his tequila bottle like a gutter rummy, and remembered the final episode in the professional life of Bernard C. Daniels. How he had crawled into Puerta del Rey more dead than alive after God knew what unspeakable happenings in the Hispanian jungle, how he drank himself back to health, and then called a press conference to announce, between hacking up blood and giggling drunkenly: "Do not fear. The CIA is here."

In five minutes, he spilled more about CIA operations than Castro had learned in five years.

Snodgrass looked at the bottle, then up at Barney.

"Forget it," Barney said, answering the question in Snodgrass's eyes. "It just happened and there isn't any why. And don't knock the tequila. God's greatest gift to tortured man."

He slid forward off the sink. "Now go home. I've got some serious drinking to do."

And Max Snodgrass, whose income tax return listed him as executive vice president of Calchex Industries, walked out of the house and drove away.

Barney wondered, as he polished off the last of the tequila and staggered back to his spot on the upstairs floor, how long the vice president of Calchex Industries would wait before having him killed.




# CHAPTER TWO


His name was Remo and he was buying dirt.

He was buying dirt because this was Manhattan, and dirt didn't come cheap here unless it was New York City dirt, the kind that blew out of automobile exhausts or sifted out of the sky or fell from the bodies of its earthier inhabitants who made their homes on the sidewalks. New York dirt was just too dirty.

Remo needed clean dirt that flowers could grow in, even though those flowers would be growing in a window of a motel room off Tenth Avenue, where they would be abandoned shortly after they were planted and replaced by candy wrappers and cigarette butts and used condoms—New York dirt.

He was not a gardener. He was an assassin, the second best assassin on the face of the earth.

The best was fifty years older than Remo, fifty pounds lighter, with fifty centuries of lethal tradition. He was the gardener.

Remo hoisted a hundred-pound plastic bag labeled Amaza-Gro onto his shoulder. According to the pressure on his deltoid muscle, it weighed exactly ninety-one pounds. Well, what the hell, Remo thought. Ninety-one pounds of dirt ought to be enough to hold down a couple of geraniums. Ninety pounds, fourteen ounces. Remo glanced down at the other bags in the pyramidal display at the back of the five and ten cent store. A golden sunburst on the front of each bag boasted that the soil was fortified with pure dehydrated Kentucky horse manure.

Remo was impressed. Imagine that. New York was getting better all the time. Dirt plus pure dehydrated Kentucky horse manure, mixed together in this plastic hundred-pound bag weighing ninety-one pounds less two ounces, for only $39.95. What a bargain. In midtown Manhattan, you could barely get a steak sandwich for that price. Then he noticed the pile of dirt on the floor where his bag of Amaza-Gro had been. He did not need to use his eyes to discern that the identical product, composed of earth, potassium sulfate, phosphorus additives, nitrogen compounds, and a heavy dose of pure dehydrated Kentucky horse manure was trickling down the right side of his black tee shirt.

"Yecch," he said aloud and tossed the bag back onto the floor. A young man wearing a cheap

15

brown suit and tinted glasses over a nose bubbling with fresh acne passed by.

"What's your problem, mister?" he sighed, slapping his blank clipboard against his thigh.

"My problem," Remo answered angrily, although he had not been angry until the pimply-faced person standing next to him opened his mouth, "is that this bag has just leaked horseshit all over me."

"So?"

With an effort of will, Remo ignored him. His boss, Dr. Harold W. Smith, a man who knew more about trouble in America than the President of the United States did, had been on Remo's back not to cause any more trouble than absolutely necessary. Unless, of course, it was in the line of duty.

"Duty" meant doing the dirty work for CURE, an organization developed by a young president years before to control crime in America by operating outside the bounds of the Constitution. He thought it was the only means left to a nation that had become so civilized, so fair, so lenient, and so dependent on the whim of lobbyists, protesters and scared politicians that it could no longer function effectively within the Constitution. CURE was dangerous. But so were America's assailants. And there were many, many assailants around the world, people, organizations and nations who despised America for its wealth and power and used its principle of fairness to cripple it.

So CURE had been created. Officially, it did not exist. Only three people on earth knew about it: the president, who passed along the knowledge of CURE to his successor. The young president who began CURE did not wait for an election to determine who his successor would be. He told his vice president, because he knew he would not live to the election, to such an extent had crime grown out of control. The young president was assassinated. But CURE would continue, so that other presidents and other Americans could live in safety.

Dr. Harold W. Smith was the second man who knew of CURE's existence. Smith worked alone in a sealed area of Folcroft Sanitarium in Rye, New York, nursing the most sophisticated computer hookup known to man, trying to treat some of America's wounds. When greedy entrepreneurs, under total Constitutional sanction, threatened to unbalance America's hair-trigger economy by cornering commodities on the stock exchange, those commodities suddenly devalued dramatically through the efforts of a thousand people who performed their regular jobs without suspecting that Smith and CURE had begun the avalanche that toppled the sandcastle.

When death stalked the streets in riots, assassinations, political plots, or organized crime waves, CURE quelled it.

When people sought to break America's back, those people were destroyed. That was CURE's main job: to destroy evil.

And there was one other man who knew about CURE, a former cop who was officially executed in an electric chair for a crime he did not commit, to begin a new life as the enforcement arm for the secret organization, a life spent in the most arduous training known to all the centuries of mankind to make him a human weapon more dangerous than a nuclear bomb.

His name was Remo.

Remo Williams.

The Destroyer.

Remo brought under control the almost overwhelming impulse to rid the young man in the five and ten cent store of the burden of existence and decided Harold W. Smith was a pain in the ass.

Killing forty-three men in broad daylight at a union rally was okay. Knocking off a fake army installation, with the arms and legs of a complete squadron of trained thugs flying dismembered through the breeze like link sausages, was peachy. But let Remo Williams pop a snotty dime store floorwalker in his acned cauliflower nose, and Smitty would be on Remo's case with razorblades for words.

Remo picked up another bag, weighing eighty-eight pounds. He picked up a third. It was also leaking. As he moved from one bag to the next, the floor beneath his loafers took on the appearance of Iowa farmland. The seventeenth bag emptied its contents at Remo's feet before it was two inches off the ground.

"This is ridiculous," Remo said. "These bags are all torn."

"You're not supposed to handle them so rough, lunkhead," the man sneered to Remo, who could count the legs on caterpillars as they walked over his hands, whose fingers had been exercised by catching butterflies in flight without disturbing the pollen on their wings. "You're just clumsy. Now look at this mess you made. You've wrecked my display. It took me three hours to set this up."

"To set me up, you mean. You knew these bags had holes in them."

"Look, it's not my job to make sure your hands don't get dirty."

"Oh yeah? What is your job, then?"

The man smiled, pushing a lock of greasy hair off his forehead, raising the curtain on another field of acne. "I'm the assistant manager, wise guy. Man-

18

ager, hear? My job is to see to it that customers take what we got, or get out. You want something, buy it. If you don't like what we stock, blow. This is New York, jerk. We don't need your business."

"Oh, excuse me," Remo said politely. To hell with Smith. "I forgot my place. I must have been thinking I was in a store, where the employees were supposed to be friendly and helpful."

The assistant manager snorted a laugh, sizing up the thin man with the abnormally thick wrists, figuring that he would bully him into buying a half-empty bag of potting soil for forty dollars, just as he had bullied his other customers into buying defective irons, soiled baby clothes, torn paperback books, dying parakeets, dented pots, and other items which customers bought because they knew they would be in approximately the same condition in other stores where the employees would be just as rude.

There was rudeness, plain old run-of-the-mill New York rudeness, and there was that special rudeness that separated the retail world from the rest of the citizenry. That special rudeness, the assistant manager knew, could not be learned. It was a gift.

The assistant manager had the gift. He was born to his calling, and he was a pro in his field. He knew how to make his customers feel so miserable, so beaten, so helpless, that they would not dare spend their money elsewhere. Since he began his job six months before, sales had gone up more than fifty percent. In another month, he would be manager. In a year, he'd be heading up the entire chain of thirty-five New York stores.

He was nearly lost in his reverie when he noticed the thin man in the dirt-spattered black tee shirt was

19

doing an amazing thing. He was picking up one of the Amaza-Gro bags with one hand. With his other hand, the thin man was wrapping a green garden hose around the assistant manager from neck to ankles. It all took place in less than three seconds.

"Just tidying up," Remo said. "Don't want you to be upset because of messy customers who dare to criticize your merchandise." He yanked the assistant manager's hair so that his eyes bulged and his mouth popped open and every follicle on his head screamed in anguish.

The assistant manager also screamed, but no one heard him because Remo had stuffed his mouth with pure dehydrated Kentucky horse manure.

"Yum, yum, eat 'em up," Remo said, kicking the assistant manager's feet out from beneath him so that he toppled to the floor and bounced on his rubber tubing exterior like a beach toy.

"Mff. Pfft," said the assistant manager.

"Beg pardon? Speak up."

"UHNNK! MMMB!"

"Seconds, you say?" Remo dumped the rest of the bag's contents into the man's mouth. Since it didn't all fit, Remo helped the Amaza-Grow through the man's quivering esophagus with a nearby trowel. The metal spade broke in two, so Remo used the handle to tamp down the dirt.

Whe the assistant manager stopped asking for more and only opened and closed his eyes in blind terror, he saw Remo do another amazing thing. With no discernible preparation, the thin man with the big wrists vaulted over aisle after aisle of factory-rejected merchandise, laying waste to the contents of the store. Broken kewpie dolls zoomed across the length of the ceiling with the speed of jet fighters. Dog-eared greeting cards sprinkled the store in a cloud of confetti. One female checkout clerk screamed The others, seeing the assistant manager immobilized, were too busy robbing the cash registers.

A very old lady, dressed in black and carrying a cane, looked up apologetically to Remo as he sailed over a pile of plastic shoes tossed randomly in a heap. The lady was holding one of the shoes in her hands, the thin sole flapping apart from the rest of the shoe.

"I didn't break it, sir," the old lady said quiveringly, offering the shoe to Remo. "It just fell apart when I touched it." She had tears in her eyes. "Please don't make me pay for these, too." Remo saw that she was wearing a similar pair on her feet, the soles held on by dozens of rubber bands. "I only wanted to see if they were all—all—" Her wrinkled old eyes crunched up around her tears. Remo grabbed the shoe away from her. It cracked and crumbled in his hand. "Lady," he asked wonderingly, "Why don't you wear sneakers? These shoes are worthless."

"I can't afford sneakers," the lady said. "Do I have to pay for the one you broke, too, sir?"

Remo reached into his pocket. "I'll let you go on two conditions," he said, handing her a wad of bills. She stared at the money in astonishment. Hundreds peeked out. "That you buy yourself a good pair of shoes, and that you never return to this store again. Got it?"

The old lady nodded dumbly. She began to totter away, but Remo pushed her gently to the side when he heard the heavy breathing of a man with an obesity problem waddling toward him three aisles away. Remo sensed from the man's uneven footfalls that he was carrying a gun. Remo waited.

21

When the manager appeared, the .38 poised amateurishly in his hand, Remo was leafing through the paperback book section, a pile of loose pages at his feet where they had fallen as the book was being opened. A sign above the books read *No Browsing*.

The man raised his gun and fired. Remo yawned. "Missed," he said.

The store manager looked unbelievingly at the gun. He had fired it point blank at Remo's chest, and he had missed. Directly behind Remo, a bullet hole smoldered through a stack of school notebooks with lines misprinted diagonally down the page.

"How'd you do that?" the manager asked. Remo felt no need to reveal the obvious: that he had moved faster than the bullet. The man fired again. Again, Remo shifted his weight off his heels, and then back onto them, and then there was another hole in the notebooks.

"This is getting dull," Remo said. And just as the fat manager was squeezing his fat finger around the trigger for the third time, he saw Remo move and decided not to shoot. As manager of a successful economy-budget chain store, he recognized his responsibility to the community. He realized that innocent people might get killed if he continued to pursue this nut case. He reconsidered shooting a defenseless man at point-blank range. He also observed that Remo had twisted the barrel of his revolver around so that it formed a perfect U and was now pointed directly into his own pudgy face.

He opened his hand to drop the gun but the gun did not drop and the hand did not open because the butt of the gun was jammed into the metacarpals of his hand. Then came the pain.

*"Eeeeeeeee,"* the manager cried.

Remo tugged at his ear and shook his head. "That's not E. That's A-flat. You tone deaf?"

"*Eeeeee,*" the man insisted.

"No, no," Remo said. "Here's E." He twisted the man's ear. The pain shot up eight notes.

Remo nodded his head approvingly. "Now I'll make the pain go away, if you'll do something in return," Remo offered.

"Anything. One—thirty-five—twenty-four—six-teen—eight."

"What?"

"That's the combination to the safe. *Eeeeeeee.*"

"Hallelujah," said one of the checkout clerks who had come to watch the action. She ran off toward the safe in the back of the store, followed by the rest of the staff.

"So much for your money," Remo said. "Now I want you to do a little advertising, to let your customers know what an honest guy you are."

"Sure, sure," the manager grunted, the veins in his neck throbbing. "Stop this . . . please."

"In a second. Right after I give you your instructions. Are you listening carefully?"

"Yes. YES!"

"I want you to stand outside this store and tell everybody on the street what kind of operation you're running. The markups, the merchandise, the help. Everything. And the whole truth, right?"

"Right." The man panted to hold down the pain in his ear and his hand, but nothing helped.

Remo escorted him to the doorway by the ear. "Okay, start talking," he said.

"Pain," the man yelped.

"Oh. Forgot." Remo released the ear and pressed a small nerve network beneath the skin on the man's wrist and the man's arm went numb. The pistol clattered to the sidewalk. He breathed in heavily with relief.

"Can you move your arm?" Remo asked.

"No."

"Good. Then it doesn't hurt. But if I don't like what you're saying, I'll make the numbness go away and the pain come back, understand?"

"Yes."

"Okay. I trust you. Talk."

"Help!" the man yelled. *Eeeeeee!*

"What'd I tell you?" Remo scolded. He touched the manager's wrist.

"B-bad merchandise," the man sputtered.

"Louder."

"Can't," the man sobbed.

Remo numbed his arm again. "Try now."

"This store has been cheating the pants off you every since it opened," the man yelled with the zeal of an evangelist. "I ought to know, I'm the manager. I buy rejected merchandise from factories and don't let you know about it when I sell it to you. All of these stores are stocked the same way."

"The clerks," Remo reminded him, smiling and nodding to the bewildered pedestrians on the sidewalk.

"The clerks are nasty as hell! You'd be crazy to shop here."

"Good work," Remo said and patted the man on the back. "Keep at it." Remo strolled back into the store. He picked up a bunch of plastic flowers and walked over to the assistant manager who was still rolled up tightly in his sarcophagus of green rubber garden hose. "Look what I brought to cheer you up," he said, and stuck the stems into the flower pot that used to be the assistant manager's mouth.

The petals fell off on contact. They just didn't

make plastic like they used to. With a flick of his foot, Remo sent the ball of garden hose containing the assistant careening to the ceiling, where it bounced spectacularly and veered off in a trajectory toward the door. It sped through the exit and came to rest exactly where Remo had planned, in the gutter in front of the manager.

"It's the worst store in New York!" the manager screamed so loud that his voiced cracked. "Maybe the world!" Remo flashed him the okay sign as he trotted past.

"It's the pits!" the manager yelled. "Save your money. Go someplace else!"

But already a small crowd was filtering through the doors, anxious to buy. After all, it was New York, and a bargain was a bargain.

Remo grumbled as he pulled back the oars on the rowboat.

"Don't go so fast," Smith said, his pinched lemon face squeezed tight against the wind as Remo plowed across the lake at forty knots. "You'll attract attention."

Indeed, a few boaters on the lake in Central Park turned their heads as the little rowboat flew past with the speed of a Harley Davidson at full throttle.

"Attract attention?" Remo looked across at his two passengers. Smith was dressed in his usual three-piece gray suit, which he would have worn even if the meeting had taken place under water. Next to Smith sat an aged Oriental, with skin like parchment and thin, cloudlike wisps of white hair on his head and face. He was swathed in a long robe of red brocade. "If this is your idea of an inconspicuous meeting place, you're nuttier than I thought you were," Remo said.

25

"Forgive him, Emperor," the old Oriental said as he flicked his frail hand from the sleeve of his kimono, displaying fingernails as long as penknives. "He is an ungrateful child who does not understand that it is his honor to propel this craft for the American emperor and the Master of Sinanju." He bowed his head toward Smith. "Also, he seeks to disguise his faulty breathing with this show of irritation."

"My breathing is perfect," Remo protested.

"As you see, Emperor, he is also arrogant. Now, if the Master of Sinanju had been given a decent specimen to train instead of a fat meat eater with skin the color of a fish belly—"

"Better watch it, Chiun," Remo cautioned. "Smitty's the white devil, too. Anyway, you're just mad because I didn't bring back the potting soil."

"You see? He admits it. This oafish person who has failed to bring his old master the one item which would have filled the master's final years with joy even brags to you that he is incompetent. And what was that item, you may ask? It was not one of your airplanes which serve inedible foodstuffs and require that one wait endlessly in line to use the lavatory. It was not a television set on which is shown violence and pornography in place of its once serene daytime dramas. No. What the Master of Sinanju had requested as the final flickering light in his twilight-dimmed life was only earth from the ground. Simple dirt, Emperor, so that I might have had the pleasure of growing bright flowers to ease the pain of my weary life."

"I told you what happened," Remo said.

"He was too occupied engaging in a senseless altercation, in which not even one individual was properly assassinated, to remember his old master."

"I know about it," Smith said flatly.

26

"Lo, Remo. All the world knows of your loutishness. An assassin who does not assassinate is a useless assassin. You are a sluggish, forgetful, and ungrateful wretch who fails even to bring a small pot of earth to an old man."

"It was disgraceful," Smith said.

"See? See?" Chiun jumped up and down in the boat delightedly. "I would be most grateful, Emperor, to accept a new pupil at your command. Maybe someone young. The right color."

"You could have been caught, Remo. You know what that would mean. The end of CURE." Smith turned his head in disgust.

Remo said nothing. He knew Smith didn't bring him out in the middle of a lake to slap his wrists.

And Smith was right. Not that Remo was bound by loyalty to CURE, as Smith was. CURE was what sent Remo out to kill people he did not even know, against whom he held no grudge. CURE was responsible for the thousand motel rooms instead of one home, for the near certainty that he would never have a woman of his own to love, or children to bear his name, for the plastic surgery that had changed his face and the unending stream of paper to change his identity.

Who was Remo Williams? Nobody. A dead policeman with an empty grave and a marker somewhere in the eastern United States. Only the Destroyer remained. And CURE.

But the end of CURE would mean the end of Smith, too. It was arranged that way. To Smitty, the prospect of his own death was just another item of information in his orderly file clerk's mind. If the president ordered CURE to be disbanded, Smith would press one button on his computer console to destroy all of CURE's information banks in sixty seconds. Then he would descend unhesitatingly to the basement of Folcroft sanitarium, where his casket and a small vial of poison waited.

For Smith, suicide was just another routine thing he would do one day when he was ordered to. But somehow, and Remo would not have been able to say why, he would miss Smitty's bitter face and acidic ways.

"What's the assignment?" Remo asked softly, breaking the silence.

"A former CIA agent named Bernard C. Daniels. He blew the lid on the agency about a year ago in Hispania."

"A double?"

"No," Smith said. "A fine operative, really, judging from his past performance. But an alcoholic now. His memory is gone. Even under hypnosis, Daniels draws a blank about the Hispania business. It seems he was sent there on a routine mission, requested an extension, disappeared for three months, and then staggered into Puerta del Rey one morning and announced the CIA presence there. A big international mess, and nobody knows anything about how it happened or why. Daniels claims the CIA tortured him. They deny it. And now that the press has forgotten him, it's time to remove him before he becomes a further embarrassment to the CIA."

"Pardon me for knocking your old alma mater, Smitty, but the CIA's an embarrassment to the CIA."

"Nobody knows that better than I do."

"Since when do we do the CIA's laundry?" Remo asked.

"Washing clothes is an appropriate task for so incompetent an assassin and so ungrateful a pupil,"

Chiun said, nodding appreciatively toward Smith.

"The agency's head of operations, Max Snodgrass, has family connections to the president. Ordinarily, I wouldn't have taken this—er—project, but I served with Snodgrass in World War II, and if he's anything like he used to be, Daniels could take out a full page advertisement in the *New York Times* before Snodgrass could manage to get rid of him. Snodgrass doesn't know about CURE or me or you, of course. As far as he's concerned, he's going to identify Daniels to a freelancer who will then take care of things."

"Identify him? Why not just give me Daniels's address?"

"Snodgrass insists on going by the book and fingering Daniels himself." Smith looked out over the water. "And so does the president."

"I thought CURE wasn't supposed to be political."

Smith allowed himself the briefest moment to think about something which was not on his day's agenda. It was a vision of the basement of Folcroft sanitarium. "We can get back to the dock now," he snapped. "This should be an easy assignment."

"Why?"

"Barney Daniels is a dinosaur at the CIA, an old-fashioned agent. He didn't use weapons, even at the peak of his career. You won't have any kind of interference. And he's an alcoholic. He'll be defenseless."

"That's a terrific incentive, Smitty. You really know how to make your employees enthusiastic about their work."

Smith shrugged. "Somebody's got to do it."

That was the reason Remo usually got when he

was sent out to kill. Somebody had to do it. Somebody had to look into a dying man's eyes and think: "That's the biz, sweetheart."

And Smith wasn't often wrong in picking Remo's targets. Usually they were vermin that Remo was glad to get rid of. On several occasions, those vermin had been deadly enough to obliterate the country, if they had been allowed to live, and on those occasions, Remo felt that he was somebody after all, that he had some purpose in life besides eliminating strangers who were someone else's enemy.

But sometimes it hurt to kill. And that was why Remo was not yet the perfect assassin, although he was the best white man there was, and why he still had 80-year-old Chiun as his teacher, and why he would kill Bernard C. Daniels very quickly and with no pain, but would think about it later.

"What happens when I get too old to work for CURE, Smitty?" Remo asked as he eased the little rowboat next to the docking platform.

"I don't know," Smith answered honestly.

"Don't plan on being a gardener if you can't even remember to bring home dirt," Chiun said.

## CHAPTER THREE

The phone rang twenty times. Twenty-one. Twenty-two. Twenty-three.

When he was certain it would ring until he either

answered it or succumbed to massive brain damage from the noise, Barney Daniels stumbled over an obstacle course of empty tequila bottles to pick up the receiver.

"What do you want," he growled.

A woman's voice, laced with southern honey, answered. "You didn't call."

"I don't love you any more," Daniels said automatically. That one usually worked with unidentifiable women.

"You don't even know me."

"Maybe that's why I don't love you."

He hung up, satisfied with a romance ended well. He should drink a toast to that romance, whoever it was with. It had probably been a glorious night. It might even have been worth remembering, but there was no chance of that now. He would give that romance a proper posthumous tribute with a drink of tequila.

Barney rooted through the mountain of empty bottles. Not a drop.

Booze-guzzling bitch, he thought. No doubt the unrememberable woman, selfish wretch that she was, had sucked up the last ounce of his Jose Macho, callously unconcerned about his morning cocktail. The whore. He was glad he was rid of her. Now he would drink a toast to having gotten rid of her. If he could only find a drink.

His eagle eye spotted an upright bottle in the corner of the room with a good half-inch left inside. Ah, the queen, he said to himself as he lumbered toward it, arms outstretched. A woman among women. He raised the bottle to his lips and accepted its soul-restoring contents.

The phone rang again. "Yes," he answered cheerfully.

31

"The CIA is going to kill you," the woman said.

"Was it wonderful for you, too?" Barney crooned.

"What are you talking about?"

"Last night."

"I've never met you, Mr. Daniels," the woman said sharply. "I called you last week, but you said you were too busy drinking to talk. You said you'd call me back."

"Call . . . me . . . unreliable," Barney sang in a shaky baritone, snapping his fingers.

"I am trying to tell you, Mr. Daniels," the woman shouted, "that you have been marked for death by the Central Intelligence Agency, your former employer."

Barney rubbed the sleep from his eyes. "You woke me up to tell me that?"

"I am calling to offer you sanctuary."

"Do you have a bar?"

"Yes."

"I'll be right over."

"In return for that sanctuary, I would like you to perform a small task for me."

"Shit," Barney said. The world was right. There was no such thing as a free lunch. He was about to hang up when the woman added, "I will pay you a thousand dollars."

"Well, well," he said, suddenly interested. There was still the better part of a month to go before his next Calchex pension check. All that remained of Snodgrass's last payment to Barney were the empty bottles on the floor.

"For one day's work," the woman continued tantalizingly.

"Provided it is very legal and above board and does not involve politics or espionage," Barney said.

Who knew that the woman wasn't a secretary in Snodgrass's office? Sneaky Snodgrass wouldn't be above doing that.

"I will discuss your work when you get here."

She gave him detailed instructions on how to reach a large brownstone building on the northern end of Park Avenue, a building just across the socially acceptable line that separates the very poor from the very rich in Fun City.

"You will arrive between midnight and one A.M. by taxi. When you get out of the taxi you will place a white handkerchief over your mouth three times. Pretend to cough. Then lower the handkerchief and walk up the stairs and stand at the door. I warn you. Don't try to approach the house any other way."

"I'm just glad we're not involved in anything illegal," Daniels said.

The woman ignored him. "Do you understand everything I've said?"

"Certainly," Barney answered. "There's only one problem."

"You'll be paid very well for your problems," the woman said.

"This problem requires money. You see, I've invested very heavily in American Peace Bonds and I am without liquid capital."

"That will be straightened out when you get here."

"That's the problem. If it's not straightened out first, I won't get there."

"You're broke?"

"Said brilliantly."

"I'll have a boy at your home in two hours."

He was the biggest boy Barney had ever seen, six-and-a-half feet tall with a shaved black head shaped

33

like a dum-dum bullet without a crease. He was muscular and the muscles apparently did not stop until they reached his toes, which were encased in golden slippers with toes curling up to a metallic point.

In the lapel button hole of his black suit he wore a gold crescent with the title *Grand Vizier* stamped on it in ersatz Arabic lettering.

"I am to escort you," said the giant.

"Where are you from?"

"The woman."

"I was supposed to receive money, not an escort," Barney said.

"I have my orders."

"Well, I don't move without cash, Ali Baba, so just hop back on your flying carpet and go tell her that."

"Will you come with me if I give you money?" The giant's eyes dripped hatred at the thought of negotiating with the white devil.

"Of course. That will indicate your good faith. That's all I'm interested in. It's not the money, naturally."

The Grand Vizier of the Afro-Muslim Brotherhood took from his jacket pocket a hundred-dollar bill. He offered it to Daniels coldly.

"One hundred dollars?" Daniels screamed, edging back into his foyer. "One hundred dollars to go all the way from Weehawken to New York? You must be out of your mind. What if I have to stop for something to eat?"

The Grand Vizier's eyes kept hating. "One hundred dollar too much for a little ride across the river. It only cost you thirty cent on the bus and another sixty cent for the subway. Maybe six buck by cab."

"That's for peasants," Daniels said and shut the door.

The gentle knocking almost shook the timbers of the large house. Daniels opened the door.

"I give you two hundred dollar."

Daniels shrugged. A man had to earn a living, and anyhow everybody cribbed on their expenses.

The Grand Vizier handed over another hundred-dollar bill. "Here," he said, and the tone of his voice made it clear that he felt Barney had come cheap, that he was just another piece of chattel whose price the Grand Vizier carried as pocket money.

Catching the implication in the Grand Vizier's voice, Barney looked into his fierce eyes and then tore the second hundred-dollar bill in half with the finesse of a courtier.

"That's what I think of your money," Barney said. He made a mental note to buy Scotch tape on the way back. Two little strips, and the bill would be good as new. "I just wanted to see how bad you needed me." When the Grand Vizier wasn't looking, Barney stuffed the two halves of the bill into his pocket. One never knew.

Their co-equal relationship established, Barney opened the door to leave with the Grand Vizier. Out of the corner of his eye, he spotted a shiny object inadequately concealed in the shrubbery. Sunlight glinted off the object, which Barney recognized as a microphone. Only one man, Barney knew, would be stupid enough to place metal equipment in the one spot of shrubbery accessible to morning sunlight. Max Snodgrass undoubtedly found the best reception there, and the CIA surveillance manual, which Snodgrass wrote, insisted that equipment be placed in a area of maximum reception.

35

"Meet me in Mickey's Pub," Barney said quietly. "Two blocks east, turn left. The right hand side."

"I permit no alcohol to enter my body," the Grand Vizier said disdainfully.

"Mickey's Pub, or I keep the two bills and don't show," Barney whispered. "And you can tell the Avon company that men's cosmetics are for faggots," he yelled for Max Snodgrass's benefit.

America, thy name is perfidy, Barney lamented as he hoisted his bulky frame through the back bedroom window and dropped fifteen feet into the overgrown tomato garden below. He landed crouched on his feet, then rolled into an easy somersault to absorb the shock. Casting off your unwanted veterans, he thought bitterly, forcing them to ply their trade for a pittance to the highest bidder. Only the vision of the woman's well-stocked bar kept him going as he crawled through the jungle of his back yard into the woods behind.

While relieving himself behind a tree, he noticed a car with two men parked near his house. One was a thin, youngish man. The other was a tiny, ancient Oriental. Max's henchmen, he thought, with no particular emotion. He would doubtless see them again.

He ambled off into the woods to take the scenic route to Mickey's Pub.


"This thing must be Emperor Smith's informant," Chiun said as Max Snodgrass, hair plastered tightly to his head, tiptoed into view from behind the shrubbery. Snodgrass looked toward the car and nodded crisply.

"Dipshit," Remo said, nodding back. "He ought to be the target instead of that poor used-up drunk inside. Anybody who combs his hair like that deserves to work for the CIA."

"It is not your duty to criticize our Emperor's commands, incompetent one," Chiun said, his papery face bland.

"Lay off, Little Father," Remo said irritably. Together they watched Snodgrass swagger up the steps to Daniels's door and ring the bell. "I hope Daniels shoots this nincompoop."

Chiun whirled around in his seat to face him. "Remo, you are indulging yourself in a dangerous game. There is nothing more deadly to an assassin than his own emotions."

"All right. Then you tell me. Why should I kill this guy?" Remo asked, his voice rising. "All he ever did was to expose the CIA as the clowns they are. Look at that cretin." Max was tapping his foot on the doormat impatiently, his hands on his hips.

"Yes. I can hear his breathing from here." Chiun clucked dispiritedly. "Nevertheless, it is not your place to ask why. You must perform the task you have been trained for, so that Emperor Smith will continue to send his yearly tribute of gold to Sinanju. Otherwise, the poor people of my village will starve and be forced to send their babies back to the sea."

"Sinanju has got to be the richest village in Korea by now," Remo said. "How many submarines full of gold does it take to keep those beanbags in your hometown from tossing their kids into the ocean, anyway? Why don't they just use the Pill?"

"Do not make light of the plight of my village," Chiun said. "Were it not for the Master of Sinanju, they would be destitute. We will do our work without complaint, difficult as that must be to one whose fat white being is marbled with willfulness and discontent." He snapped his jaws shut and was still.

37

Max Snodgrass shrugged after ten minutes in front of the door and headed toward the car. Remo revved up the engine.

"I suppose James Bond is going to come over for a little chat now," Remo said. "He probably wants to let us in on the top secret information that Daniels isn't home." Remo waited. He wanted to peel away just as Snodgrass approached the car, so that the wake of gravel and dust would splatter over Snodgrass's expensive suit.

But Snodgrass stopped halfway, looking intently at Daniels's mailbox. He opened it. There was a letter inside, a big thick one in a chartreuse-colored envelope. Gingerly he whisked it out. From the car, Remo could see a name in the upper left corner.

A look of shock came over Snodgrass's face as he stared at the name. His face seemed to say it couldn't be. It couldn't be.

The name on the envelope was important to Max Snodgrass, because it was to be the last thought he ever had. At the very moment when the synapses in Max Snodgrass's brain were vibrating the language code for that name, the green envelope in his hand was exploding with the force of two sticks of dynamite and sprinkling the flesh of Max Snodgrass across the lawn like pieces of shish kebab.

"Daniels, you old rummy, you did it," Remo said. He turned on his windshield wipers to clean the red debris off the window.

"Very sloppy," Chiun said, his nose wrinkled in disgust. "A boom destroys the purity of the assassin's art. This Daniels is also a loutish white fool, I see."

"You mean bomb," Remo said. "And I hear the police." He dropped the car into gear.

38

"One moment." Chiun opened the door and rose slowly. "Sitting in an automobile is most unpleasant for the hip joints."

"This is no time to stretch your legs, Little Father. We don't want to have to murder the entire Weehawken police force."

"The police are still a quarter-mile away," Chiun said, and then whirred through the mess of Snodgrass's remains with a speed so fast even Remo could not follow all of his moves. "The police are now two hundred yards in the distance," Chiun said, returning to the car. "Let us leave, Remo."

Remo tore down the street and onto the highway, the sirens growing faint behind him.

"What'd you do back there, Chiun?" Remo asked as he turned onto a dirt road and slowed to ninety.

The old Oriental uncurled his delicate hand, revealing a pile of small pieces of green paper, their edges charred brown. "These are from the envelope which contained the boom." He turned the pieces over, one by one. "Some have writing on them. This one has a name. It says 'Denise Daniels.' Who is that?"

"I don't know," Remo said, "but it sure seemed important to Snotlocker or whatever his name was. We'll send it to Smith. And it's bomb." Chiun put the pieces inside the folds of his robe.

"This looks like the place," Remo said as he and Chiun entered the side door of Mickey's Pub, its windows decorated with dirt and neon shamrocks.

"The stink of it assaults the nostrils," Chiun said. "I shall slow my breathing so as to inhale as little of this unwholesome odor as possible."

Inside, a dozen fat, pink-faced men were enter-

39

taining themselves at the bar with jokes about the unusual footwear of a tall black man standing at the other end of the bar, drinking ginger ale.

Remo and Chiun wound their way across the floor, littered with peanut shells and broken pretzels, to a sticky table in the far corner.

"Is this indeed the restaurant at which this American person, Daniels, partakes of his meals?" Chiun asked, incredulous.

"That's what Smitty says. But he doesn't eat. He just drinks."

"How long must we wait in this iniquitous sink?"

"Till he shows up, I guess."

"Perhaps I will return to the car."

"Hold it, Chiun, that's him coming in now. The one in the white suit." Remo indicated Daniels, whose appearance was only slightly more presentable than it had been in the newspaper photograph taken after he had emerged from three months in the Hispanian jungle.

Daniels sat next to the Grand Vizier. The men at the bar stared. They were dressed in rough checkered shirts, with short jackets and dirty fedoras whose years of internal sweat had clearly overwhelmed their sweat bands and stained the hats a darker shade. They all drank beer, slowly enough so that the foam was left in rings down toward the bottom of the glass where the beer looked dead and yellow.

As the Grand Vizier stared stonily into his glass of ginger ale, the white men discussed the worthlessness of some persons who only liked to drink, fornicate and fight. That was all some persons were good for.

This concept intrigued Barney and he asked if any of the gentlemen at the end of the bar had personally developed a polio vaccine, discovered penicillin, invented the radio, discovered atomic power, invented writing, discovered fire or made any great contributions to the thought of man.

The men at the other end of the bar disclosed that the late President John F. Kennedy was not black.

Barney informed them that not only was President Kennedy not black, he was not related to the men at the end of the bar any more than he was to Barney's tall black friend.

They said that perhaps the president was not related to them but that Barney obviously was related to his dark friend. This, they thought, was very funny. So did Barney, who said that for a minute the men had given him a fright because he thought he might have been related to them instead of to the Grand Vizier, who knew how to dress like a human being, which they did not. Then he inquired of them which ditches they had dug and if any of them had seen their wives sober in the last decade.

For some reason the discussion seemed to end there with someone throwing a punch in the cause of Irish womanhood, honest labor and killing the dirty nigger lover. It was a magnificent fight. Bottles, chairs, fists. Fast. Furious. Destruction. Courage.

Barney watched every minute of it, and the Vizier did himself proud. Single-handedly, he seemed to be able to fend off the entire population of the establishment. Chairs broke over his head, fists smashed into his nose, broken bottles drew blood. But the Vizier did not fall, and continued to drop men with single strokes of his oaken arms.

Barney would have liked to have seen the finish of the fight and to tell the Grand Vizier what a magnificent man he was, but this was impossible since he was already out the front doors of the saloon, and knew that it was only a matter of seconds before the thin young man and the old Oriental seated in the far corner would be able to fight their way through the melee to get to him.

# CHAPTER FOUR

Remo blocked a body that came flying toward him. "Excuse me," he said to two men who were punching one another's faces. They did not move out of the way. "Excuse me," he said again.

"This'll excuse you," one of the men said, directing a left hook at Remo. Remo caught the man by the wrist and snapped it in half.

"Aghhhh!" the man screamed.

"Hey," the other man yelled, grabbing the back of Remo's tee shirt. "What do you think you're doing to my buddy?"

"This," Remo said, breaking the man's wrist in two between his thumb and index finger.

"I seen that," another man shouted, charging Remo with a pool cue. He swung it over his head and brought it down full force over where Remo was standing, but the stick missed its target and before he knew it the man was lifted in an arc toward the ceiling and then was crashing into the display of bottles at the back of the bar.

Bernard C. Daniels, smiling benignly in the doorway, arched an eyebrow in approval at Remo's barfighting abilities.

Remo did not acknowledge it, although he felt a small flush of pride at the subtle display of admiration. Almost everyone who saw Remo in action was either awestruck or terrified, except for Chiun, who could find flaws in even the most perfectly timed maneuver. Rarely did Remo get a sincere "well done" from anybody, and even if this one had been from a man whose life he was going to snuff out in less than thirty seconds, it felt good.

A thankless job, Remo thought as he lodged the bridgework of a man wielding a gallon jar of pickled eggs into his gums. Shrieking the man threw the jar onto a nearby table where it splintered into a thousand glass shards. The mauve-colored eggs inside rolled onto the floor, causing a half dozen men to slip and fall and continue battling one another lying down.

Then came a high-pitched wail so piercing, so pitiful, that Remo had to take his eyes off Barney Daniels, who still stood in the doorway.

It was Chiun, leaning crookedly against the bar near where the Grand Vizier stood battle, a heap of unconscious men at his feet. "Remo," Chiun cried. The front of the old man's red kimono was stained dark. "Remo," he said again, his voice a gasp.

Remo broke the legs of a man who stood in his way. He sent bodies flying across the room with his feet. He hacked his way through the crowd, dropping men like bowling pins, the panic inside him boiling to his core.

"I am here, Little Father," he said softly, picking up the old man as if he were a small child. How light his bones are, Remo thought as he raced outside with his precious bundle, weightless as bird's feathers.

Outside, he placed Chiun carefully on his back on the sidewalk. The old man's eyelids fluttered. "That was the worst experience of my life," Chiun said, shuddering.

"I swear I'll kill every last one of them. How bad is it?"

"How bad is what?" Chiun asked.

"The wound," Remo said.

"Wound? Wound?"

Slowly, Remo opened the kimono where the deep red stain was.

"What—Remo—stop that, you animal," Chiun sputtered, slapping Remo's hands.

"I have to see, Little Father." Remo pulled the kimono open over a flash of intact yellow skin.

Chiun bounded to his feet, his eyes bulging. "You have become insane!" he screeched, jumping up and down wildly, the wisps of white hair on his head streaming out behind him. "The stench of that vile place has turned you into a pervert." He clapped his hands over his sunken cheeks. "And you choose to perform your odious acts with me, with the Master of Sinanju himself. Oh, crazy one, this is the end. You have gone too far now."

He stomped off, spitting on the ground and cursing his fate to have wasted so many years on a pupil who dared to attempt the unspeakable with his own master.

"Chiun—Chiun," Remo called, racing after him. "I only wanted to see where you were hurt."

"Hurt! My heart is broken. My very soul has been desecrated. You attempted to disrobe the Master of Sinanju on a public sidewalk. Oh, this day, this day is cursed. Never should I have arisen this day. First a foul-smelling meat eater tosses purple egg juice onto my hand-woven kimono. Then my own son— no. Not my son. A perverted white man whom I was duped into believing was my good creation, whom I nurtured and taught the secrets of ages. With his own hands, this white beast dares to expose my very flesh on the street. In the debris of a saloon. Oh, shame. The house of Sinanju will never recover from this shame."

"Egg juice?"

"As I was defending myself from the lunatic assault of a drunken person with a bottle, a sea of putrid purple egg juice struck my garment. This is a foul day, a day I shall never be able to forget." He shook his head.

"You mean you're not wounded?"

"I am deeply wounded. Grievously, irreparably wounded. I must go now to burn incense and seek purification."

"Wait here." Remo ran back to the tavern, where a multitude of uniformed policemen had gathered to escort the customers into a waiting paddy wagon. He checked the wagon, and he checked the bar, but Daniels was gone.

"I've lost him," Remo said. "I lost my target because of your egg juice. I just blew my assignment."

"Do not speak to me, perverted one," Chiun said as he strode briskly toward their parked car. "I wish to be returned to my flowerless domicile, where I will make preparations to return to my village and accept the dishonor that has befallen the House of Sinanju."

"Chiun, will you please calm down? I wasn't trying to expose you. I thought you were bleeding, that's all. I didn't know you'd go to pieces over a pickled egg."

45

"Ugh. The very thought of a pickled egg is revolting. And my kimono is destroyed. It must be burned."

"You have at least a hundred more."

"And if a mother who has five children sees one of them drowned in egg juice, does she say merely that she has four others and blot the fifth child from her memory? This was my favorite robe. It is irreplaceable. And all for your silly assignment, which you did not even complete successfully. It should not have been difficult to assassinate a man whose belly had been recently stuffed with bloody beef, white bread, and fountains of alcohol."

"How do you know what he eats?"

"I smelled it."

"In the bar?"

"No, no. Idiot. One could smell nothing in that place to compare with its own stomach-shattering fragrances. I smelled it outside, just before you attempted to display my belly to the world."

"Outside where?"

"Fool. On the fire escape. Great billows of bloody beef and an alcoholic beverage based on mesquite were emanating from his mouth. Had your breathing been adequate, you could have perceived it as well."

Remo looked at the fire escape platform just above the front door.

"The fire escape? You saw him up there?"

"Why are you constantly amazed by what I say?" Chiun screamed. "I told you he was on the fire escape. Therefore, I obviously saw him. Perhaps you should join the ranks of your CIA. A person of your intelligence should be most welcome there."

Remo exhaled deeply. "I don't believe it," he said. "I just don't believe it. You knew I had to get

46

to Daniels. You saw Daniels. And you didn't tell me."

"It is not my responsibility to do your smelling for you," Chiun sniffed. "You have evidently grown so obtuse and perverted that you cannot even summon your olfactory senses to assist you. A fine assassin. Nothing but a thug. Why should I strain my powers to assist a thug in eliminating such a magnificent specimen of a man?"

"Wait a minute. Two hours ago, you were telling me that Daniels was just another target, just another mission for the good of Sinanju."

"I said nothing of the kind."

"You did too, Chiun."

"Then I have changed my mind. Your Mr. Daniels is a great man. A superb man. His leap to the fire escape was astonishing, for one who has tortured his body for so long."

"I don't get it," Remo said. "Did he see you?"

"Of course. One does not look upon the glory of Sinanju without notice."

"What did he do when he saw you?"

"Do? Why, he did only what was proper and fitting. He saluted me."

"I see. Thanks. Thanks a very large pile, Chiun. He could be dangerous, you know."

"So could you, former son, if you had not grown fat and slothful and still knew how to treat the Master of Sinanju with respect to his person."

"One salute. You let him get away for one cheap little salute."

"It was a sign of respect," Chiun said stubbornly. "Also a work of art."

"Oh, come on. Now that's really too much. A work of *art*! A work—"

"The salute was performed while Mr. Daniels

47

balanced on the balls of his feet, exquisitely, on the railing of the fire escape, out of the way of the window up there."

"Big deal," Remo said, opening the car door for Chiun.

"And he was dancing. The dance of the wind." Chiun demonstrated, his arms waving at his sides, his head turning slow circles.

"That's not dancing. That's weaving. Daniels was drunk as a pig." He slammed the door.

"Oh, to have had this specimen as a youth. To have been able to pass on the wisdom of Sinanju to one who dances even while poisoned, instead of a crazed pervert who desires to undress his master in the street."

They were silent all the way back to the motel. "Are you going to fix dinner?" Remo asked.

"Why should I eat? My body has already been desecrated."

"Okay, I'll fix dinner."

"What a specimen," Chiun reminisced, smiling dreamily. He saluted the wall.

"I wish you'd quit this."

Chiun sighed. "It was only an old man's remembrance of his one brief moment of recognition in this disrespectful world," he said. He saluted again.

The phone rang. "Please answer the telephone, Remo," Chiun said. "I am too worn and broken to exert myself."

Remo snorted. "You know I always answer the phone."

It was Smith.

"Have you completed the assignment?" he asked, his voice tense.

"No. Thanks to the Master of Sinanju and his appreciation of alcoholic ballet, I have not."

"Good."

"Good?"

"You see." Chiun interjected. "It is not only I who appreciates this fine human. The emperor also sees his grace and seeks to reward him for it."

"You've got to keep him alive," Smith said.

"What for?"

"Because someone's trying to kill him."

"Yeah. I am."

"Not any more. That envelope you couriered to me was made from paper fabricated in Hispania. There's some kind of connection. I can't get a fix on Denise Daniels yet, but that could take a while. Anyway, if somebody is trying to kill Daniels, it may be that he knows something—something of value to the U.S. That being the case, he ought to be kept alive until we know what he knows."

"This is crazy. I was supposed to kill Daniels, but now that somebody else is trying to kill him, I've got to save him. Maybe that makes sense to you, Smitty, but it doesn't make sense to me."

"Just let him do what he wants to do. Maybe it will stir the pot. But keep him alive. And Remo?"

"What?"

"That was good work, remembering to pick up the pieces of paper from the envelope."

Remo looked over to Chiun, who was saluting passersby on the street below with a jaunty flick of his wrist. "Thanks," Remo said. He hung up.

Chiun was beaming.

"I'm glad you're having such a good time," Remo said. "Personally, none of this makes any sense to me."

"It makes perfect sense, brainless one." Chiun leaped to his feet as lightly as a cloud. "All emperors are crazy, and Smith is the craziest of them all. I will cook dinner."

He padded toward the kitchen humming a tuneless Korean melody.

# CHAPTER FIVE

Bernard C. Daniels awoke in a flophouse two doors down from Mickey's, his home being three blocks away and therefore too far to walk after several days of riotous drinking throughout the town of Weehawken.

He rummaged around in his pockets. The two hundred dollars was missing. Well, I hope I enjoyed some of it, he thought as he scratched the tracks of a flea that had made its home on his scalp.

Then he discovered something that made him feel very sad. His credit at Mickey's Pub was no longer good.

He should have asked the Grand Vizier for more. But then, that would have been gone by now, too, he realized.

"What day is it?" he asked the bartender.

"It's Friday, Barney."

He looked at the luminous clock over the bourbons, scotches and ryes which rested atop planks of wood where the bar's mirrors had been. It read 8:30. It was already dark outside. "I'd better go," he said.

If he didn't hurry for his appointment with the woman, he would be late. Four days late instead of three.

The cab fare came to $4.95.

Barney handed the driver a five-dollar bill the bartender had lent him. The driver swiveled his big neck, rolled and folded to resemble the Michelin Tire Man, and yelled after him: "You promised me a big tip. I never would have came to this here neighborhood for a nickel."

Bernard C. Daniels could not be bothered with boorish taxi drivers, not amid the squalor surrounding him.

He checked the number on the building. It was correct. It was wedged between unending rows of dirty, drab brownstones. Every window on the block appeared dark, hiding faded shades and curtains, when there were curtains.

A weak street light glowed like a lonely torch high above the garbage cans and metal gratings that protected cellars. A single dog scurried with undue noise across the black-topped gutter. Traffic lights blinked their useless signals.

Barney heard the cab pull away as he mounted the steps. It left with a grumble.

The brownstone seemed identical to the others until Barney noticed the door and discovered it was only a distant relative of those stench-filled houses surrounding it.

His knock told him. There was no doorbell. Only a thin layer of the door was wood. The knock sounded like steel, extremely heavy steel. Then Bar-

51

ney noticed that the windows were not really openings to the street at his level. There were venetian blinds, all right, but they were permanently mounted on steel sheets that closed up the window.

He knocked again.

His instinct warned him, but only a split second before he felt the gentle point against his back. How many times had he felt that tender prelude to pain, that first searching of a man unsure of his blade? If he had thought, he might not have done what he did. But years of survival did not allow the mind time to think. There was a point at which the body took over, dictating its demands.

Without will, Barney's right hand slashed around, twisting his body down and away from the blade and finding a target for the line of bone from his pinky tip to his wrist. It was a black temple. It cracked with a snapping sound.

The man's head took off, followed by his neat small body encased in a neat black suit. The spectre tottered momentarily, then fell backward and would have tumbled down the steps, but for more than a dozen men identically dressed in neat black suits.

They were packed into the staircase behind him and the mass of their bodies caught their comrade.

A small bright blade with bluish edges tinkled beneath their feet on the stone steps. They all held similar blades. And they closed in on Barney almost noiselessly, a sea of shaven skulls making waves under the yellow light of the street lamp.

Barney pressed his back to the metal door and prepared to die.

Just then, two men moving so fast they were little more than blurs shot out of the darkness and into the moving sea of shining black heads.

In an instant, the quiet street was filled with

screams and the groans of dying men as blade after shimmering blade dropped to the ground and bodies twisted like wire fell on top of them.

For Barney, it was a vision of hell, witnessing the torment of men convulsed by pain and glad to die in order to end that pain.

Barney thought about that pain as he fired up a cigarette and winked at the two white men who were causing it. Better them than me, he thought philosophically.

But one of the men was not white. He was an aged Oriental sporting a turquoise kimono. "Jesus Christ," Barney muttered.

It was all very confusing to him. Here were two guys, the same two guys he was sure were out to hit him, saving his life. And fighting like bastards to boot. He had never seen fighting like that. It was effortless, artful, utterly economical of movement, totally effective. Were it not for the carnage surrounding them, the young white man and the old Oriental could have been dancing a ballet.

Very confusing. He would have to think about this matter. He would think about it immediately, in fact, just as soon as he had a drink of tequila to help him think better.

As the two men silenced the last of the mob, Barney rose to dust himself off. His eyes followed the movements of the men as they dashed out of sight. The thin young man disappeared like a bullet. The old Oriental followed, his robe floating behind him.

But just as Barney was preparing to knock again, the Oriental returned. Standing beneath the street lamp, grinning broadly, the old man stiffened like a tiny tin samurai soldier and flicked Barney an elegant salute.

"Thank you, sir," Barney said, his voice echoing

down the street, and returned the salute. Then the old man was gone.

Barney knocked twice more. After a long silence, the door surrendered and opened to him over a field of white plush carpeting. Standing at the door was the Grand Vizier of the Afro-Muslim Brotherhood, two flesh-colored Band-Aids decorating his forehead. Flesh-colored here meant brown, but against the Vizier's eggplant skin, the two strips of tape stood out like an accusation.

"Am I late?" Barney asked.

"What you done?" the Grand Vizier yelled, looking out over the heap of broken bodies in the street. One of the Vizier's large black hands came down to Barney's right shoulder and lifted him like a toy.

"Leave him alone, y'hear?" came a woman's voice. "I'll take care of him, Malcolm."

"Yes, ma'am," the Grand Vizier said and allowed Barney's feet to touch the floor.

She wore white slacks and a white blouse and Barney almost couldn't see her because of the camouflage. The whole interior of the building, fireplace, sofa, lamps, walls, ceiling, steps leading upstairs, all were painted blinding white. Marble, wood and cloth, all as white as the inside of a bathtub factory run amok with hospital orders.

Her platinum hair fit the decor perfectly. Barney shook his head as if to clear it. There was something about her. Something. He tried to think but couldn't.

Malcolm, the Grand Vizier, stood out, as he left the room, like an ink blot on a snowy towel. In the room, a faint fragrance of lilacs replaced the stink of garbage outside. Barney sniffed. He preferred the garbage.

"Beautiful," said the woman, peeking out the

54

door. She reached for a telephone, which was hidden by its absence of color, on a white table Barney could barely make out against the white wall.

"Yes," she said. "Yes. Tell them, Malcolm, that their friends have all gone to Allah and will be rewarded there. Don't forget to mention that it was a white devil who killed them. Very good. Was it clean? Immediate death? Good. Well done, Malcolm."

Barney heard, rather than saw, her hang up. She smiled, a pale, thin-lipped smile. "You killed all those men out there."

"I had some help," Barney admitted. "A hundred-year-old Chinaman did most of it."

The woman laughed. "You're charming," she said. "And the rest of the Peaches of Mecca will be impressed."

"The what?"

"The Peaches of Mecca. The bodyguard of a new revolution, a freedom movement so sweeping it astounds the imagination and thrills the soul. Of course, you just wiped out most of the Peaches. We'll have to get some new recruits."

"Got a drink?"

"You're a cold, hard professional, aren't you? Money is your grounds for loyalty, isn't it? You're cool, precise, knowledgeable about espionage, death, and destruction. You think only of the dollar and the power it gives you, isn't that right?"

"Sure. Got a drink?" he repeated.

She walked over to a well-camouflaged white bar. "What'll you have?" she asked.

"Tequila." The very word touched his heart.

She poured him a tumbler full of very expensive Bolivian firewater and handed it to him.

"You have quite a reputation for being a competent agent, Mr. Daniels," she said.

He poured the contents of the glass down his grateful throat. "Agents with reputations are not competent, madam. They are dead. May I have another?" He held up the glass.

"Of course. I want you to know before we begin, Mr. Daniels, that you will always have a drink waiting for you in my home."

"That's real southern hospitality, ma'am," Barney said smoothly, accepting his second drink.

"Anytime you want one, you just come on over and help yourself to my bar, hear?"

"Yes'm."

"Even if I'm not at home, I will leave instructions that you be admitted anytime you need a little drinky-poo."

"I'll remember that, ma'am."

She smiled at him like a sleek white cat. "I'm sure you will, Mr. Daniels."

She sat down next to him on a white sofa. "That was clever, what you said about agents with reputations being dead."

"Pleased to hear it, ma'am."

"Because you're going to be dead soon."

"So you tell me."

"Unless I help you. And I plan to help you."

"That's right neighborly. How's about a little blast?" He offered her his empty glass again. "Tequila," he said.

"In a minute. We want to talk first."

"We do?"

"What do you think the black man wants, Mr. Daniels?"

Barney furrowed his brow in concentration.

56

"Can't say I know which black man you're talking about, ma'am," he said.

"You're a bigot, Mr. Daniels." Her eyes flashed. "You don't know anything about the freedom movement, and you don't care."

"I resent that," Barney said, rising. He eased his way toward the bar. "I care about freedom as much as anybody. There is nothing more important to me than freedom. At this very moment, in fact, the prospect of receiving a free drink from your bar is foremost in my mind."

"You get back here. Come back to this couch this second, or I'll order Malcolm to smash every bottle in the house."

"I'm coming, I'm coming." He sat down, his empty glass clutched in his hand.

"You are a backward, white liberal bigot who doesn't understand the freedom movement. So I will explain it to you."

"I was afraid of that," Barney mumbled.

"It's the great spirit rising from the newly emerged nations of Africa. It's written on the wind. The black man is pure. Untrammeled by white corruption, untouched by either communism or capitalism. He is the future."

Barney sensed movement in the tightly wrapped milk-colored stretch pants and the full blouse that tightened at the waist. "What's so pure about him?" he asked, managing to tear his gaze from the sight of the woman's full bouncing breasts.

"He never had a past. The white man robbed him of it."

"Certainly," Barney said, as though seeing for the first time in the light shed by this dizzy daffodil. Nevertheless, surrounding this ripe albino plant was green, green money, all watered by liquor. The black man was pure, yes indeedy. Barney couldn't argue with that.

"He's like writing on a clean blackboard," Barney offered.

"Exactly," said the woman, flowering with sudden happiness. "He's been robbed, whipped, raped, castrated, and ciphered as a human being."

Barney nodded knowingly. "That'd make anyone pure," he said.

"Right. Perhaps I was wrong about you, Mr. Daniels. Perhaps you are interested in more than money."

"But of course," Barney said gallantly. "I never would have come here if I didn't believe I would be working for a good cause."

"Ah, wonderful. A man who wants more than money. Good. We're running short of funds now anyhow."

Barney started for the door.

"Stop," the woman called, wedging herself between Barney and the door before he could locate the white doorknob. "We have plenty of money. Millions," she yelled into his face.

"Millions?" Barney asked.

"Millions." She pulled him toward her. He attempted to fight his way free, but his left hand which was reaching for the door drew itself inexplicably around her waist instead. And his right hand somehow began playing brazenly with her jiggling breast and his lips were laboring above, working their independent way from her mouth down her neck to her erect pink nipples, and oh, goodness gracious, her pants were coming off.

"Take me upstairs and make love to me," she whispered hoarsely.

58

"Yes, yes," Barney obeyed, lifting her off the smooth carpeting and heading directly for the stairwell with only a small detour to the bar to pick up a bottle.

In the round white bed, Barney worked his hands over the woman's silky body. She teased his ear with her teeth.

"You will kill for me," she hissed, fired with passion.

"Yeah," Barney said.

She pulled him on top of her. "You'll spy for me."

"Yeah."

"You'll do anything I say." With agonizing slowness, she opened her legs to him.

"Yeah."

"Anything."

"You name it," Barney said, bringing her to full gallop.

"Anything," she moaned.

With intoxicating relief, Barney spent himself. "Well, almost anything, honey," he said, puffing. "Can't rush into things, you know."

She was mad, but not too mad. About as mad as a satisfied woman can get. "Roll over," she said, tweaking his cheek.

Barney did, and his eye fell on the bottle he had brought up with him. It was bourbon. What the hell, he thought. He would start cultivating a taste for the stuff. It was easier than trekking nude past Malcolm to retrieve the tequila.

"Forgot the glasses."

"Drink from the bottle. Give me a cigarette." She sat up in bed, her firm, sharp breasts peering out above the sheets. Barney handed her a pack of smokes.

59

He took a swig. It went down hot and good. It was fine bourbon. There was much to be said about the drink.

"How about me?" the woman asked. She extended her hand for the bottle.

Barney examined the hand. It had fine lines. It was a fine hand. If he had another bottle of bourbon, he certainly would have put it into that hand.

"Well, how about me?"

It was a good question. Barney took another swallow, a long one. She had a right as his bed partner to share in the bourbon. An inalienable right. She certainly had that right. And it was her bourbon. Barney swallowed again and moved her hand away.

She settled for a cigarette. They lay back contentedly, she smoking, Barney drinking, and she told him about the Afro-Muslim Brotherhood.

Her name was Gloria X and she was its leader although only a handful of people knew it. It was a secret society aimed at fomenting a sense of outrage among the black people, to make them angry enough to revolt against their white oppressors.

"Enough, enough," Barney said, waving away her prepared speech. "What is it you want me to do? Paint my face with shoe polish and join the Peaches of Mecca?"

"I want you to kill someone."

"Anyone special?"

"A prominent civil rights leader whose middle-of-the-road policy is holding back the cause of black nationalism and the freedom movement."

"How do you know I won't go racing off to the police with this information?"

"Because, Mr. Daniels." She smiled evilly.

"Because what?"

She stared directly into his eyes, her coldness reaching to the pit of Barney's stomach. "Because I know what happened in Puerta del Rey. That's an interesting scar you carry," she said, touching the "CIA" brand on his belly.

Barney turned toward her. He was about to speak. He was about to tell her that he himself did not remember what happened in Hispania that led him through the jungle and into the hut where he had been tied and cut and burned with the glowing poker, that he did not remember the thing buried deep in his brain, the event that caused him not to care when they cut him and beat him and branded him and yet kept him alive in spite of the torture.

He was going to tell her, but she cut him off. "So I know, Mr. Daniels, that you have no love for this government or its agencies or, for that matter, for white men."

So she didn't know. She didn't know any more than he did.

"And besides, Mr. Daniels," she continued, "if you refuse I will have you killed. Now, hush up. The news is coming on."

Gloria X flipped a switch at the bed table and a transistorized television set on the opposite wall instantly lit up.

Barney sipped the bourbon, once again trying to remember Hispania but failing, as always. Something had happened there. Something.

The newscast reported on the usual goings on of the planet. A revolution in Chile, a flood in Missouri. A drought threatened in New Jersey, and a civil rights threat in New York.

Gloria X began to emit happy little squeals as the television flashed a picture of a fat black man. Daniels had seen him several times on TV in South

America. He was called a national civil rights leader. He spoke a lot, but was never shown with a following of more than forty persons, most of them white Episcopal ministers.

He was Calder Raisin, national director of the Union of Racial Justice, commonly called URGE, fat, pompous, invariably making wild inaccurate statements calculated to offend whites and at best amuse blacks who paid him no attention anyway.

The affected voice bellowed out of the TV set. "The Block Mon," Raisin shouted, "will not tolerate lily-white hospital staffs. At least one out of every five doctors must be black, in both public and private hospitals." It took Barney a while to understand that "Block Mon" meant "black man." Maybe Raisin's gulping adenoidal pronunciation was a new proof of high culture.

"Mr. Raisin," the television reporter quizzed, "where will the country get all these black doctors?"

"After centuries of educational deprivation, the Block Mon must be given doctor's degrees. I demahnd a massive medical education program for Blacks, and, if need be, an easing of the discriminatory standards of medical boards."

"Would you name these discriminatory standards?"

"I would be glad to. Because of segregated and inferior education, the Block Mon has more difficulty getting into medical school, let alone passing tests given by white medical boards of examination.

"I demahnd immediate abolition of entrance examinations for medical schools. I demahnd the end of testing to pass. I demahnd the end of the strict standards of medical schools as just another technique of Jim Crow segregation, northern style."

"And if your demahnds—er, demands—are not met by the medical schools?" the reporter asked.

"We shall begin a sick-in, utilizing every badly needed hospital bed. I call upon everyone, Block Mon and white alike, who has a passion for racial justice to register at a hospital. I have here a list of phony symptoms guaranteed to get you admitted. When the truly sick are dying in the streets because there are no beds for them, perhaps then the medical schools will face up to the need to create more black doctors."

The camera panned back, revealing the portly Mr. Calder Raisin clad in a white hospital gown, standing by an empty bed. His voice was taken off the audio and a commercial for throat lozenges went on.

"Oh. Oh," squealed Gloria X. "He's great. Great. Just great. Great."

With each great, Barney felt her squeeze a tender spot of his anatomy.

"Great," Gloria X said.

Barney pinched her hand. She ignored the pinch. "Great, he was great, darling. Wasn't he wonderful?"

Barney sipped the bourbon and grunted. "He's not my type."

"Well, he is mine," Gloria X said. "He's my husband."

Barney looked at her.

She leaned over, brushed the bottle away from Barney's mouth onto the floor, and ran her tongue over his lips.

"He's really great," she whispered. "It's a shame you're going to have to kill him."

Barney pushed her away from him. "Now wait a

second. First you tell me you're married to this chocolate donut—"

Gloria nodded. "He's great," she said.

"And then you tell me to go out and kill him."

She smiled.

"May I ask why?" he said after a pause.

"To further the cause of black freedom," she said. "To eliminate Raisin's middle-of-the-road policy from the rising black consciousness. To demonstrate to my followers that personal sacrifice in the cause of freedom is glorious—"

"And to collect the insurance money?"

"It's a bundle, big boy." She winked.

"That's what I thought," Barney said. He took a deep swig from the bourbon bottle and rolled away from her.

# CHAPTER SIX

The Grand Vizier of the Afro-Muslim Brotherhood held open the door for Barney as he tiptoed out of Gloria X's house at five in the morning.

"Thanks, Malçolm," he said, trying not to slur his words too much.

"Once you out on the street, you ain't my problem," Malcolm answered. "Plenty of bloods be happy to see your white face this time of day. Ain't no way Allah be looking out for you, white scum."

"Hare Krishna," Barney said with a bow.

Barney wasn't afraid of muggers. He could still

fight when he had to. He wasn't afraid of killers. He had killed too many times himself not to know that killers were generally more frightened than their victims unless the killers were very well trained, and if the Peaches of Mecca were the best fighting men in the neighborhood, he was in no danger. And, with nothing in his pocket but the five-dollar bill Gloria X had given him to insure his return, he wasn't particularly afraid of getting robbed.

What Barney Daniels was afraid of was that crazy old Oriental guy who seemed to materialize magically on the dim street corner ahead. He prepared to run in the opposite direction, but the old man was standing beside him before Barney could execute the about-face.

"You sure are fast, Pops," Barney said.

"Thank you. Greetings. I am Chiun."

"Barney Daniels."

"Yes, I know."

"Where's your friend?"

"He is nearby."

Barney looked around him, but saw no one. "I don't mean to be nosy, Chiun, but are you planning to kill me?"

"No."

Barney breathed easier. "That's good. You know, Chiun, for some reason you don't look like you live in the neighborhood."

"I do not. My home is the village of Sinanju, in Korea."

"I see," Barney said, as though that explained everything. "Going my way?"

"Yes." They walked silently for another half block.

Barney tried again. "Listen, I know this sounds weird, but—"

"Yes?"

"No, it's too weird."

"Go ahead. You may ask."

"Okay." He felt foolish even thinking it. "It's just that I saw you fight. You were pretty good, know what I mean?"

Chiun smiled. "It was nothing."

"So I was wondering, if you can fight like that, and if you're not going to kill me, well . . ."

"Yes?"

"Are you my fairy godfather or something?"

A voice behind him snickered. Barney jumped into the air, his heart thudding. "Good reflexes," Remo remarked.

"How long have you been back there?"

"Since you left the house."

Barney shook his head. "You two are really something," he said, extending his hand to Remo. "Barney Daniels."

"Idi Amin," Remo said, declining the hand.

"One of us is the Master of Sinanju," Chiun elaborated. "The other is a rude pervert who is barely useful for household tasks."

"And the third is a drunk we've had to stay up all night watching while he humped his way to heaven," Remo growled.

"How could you watch?"

Remo shrugged. "No scruples, I guess."

"I mean, the sides of the building were sheer faces of poured concrete. You couldn't have looked in the window."

"Suit yourself."

"What did you hear?" Barney asked, testing.

"Nothing special. Grunts, groans, a couple of giggles from Blondie, a belch or two from you—the usual."

"Hmmm."

"And your promise to knock off Calder Raisin for her."

Barney winced. "You from the CIA?" he asked.

"That does it," Remo said. "He's going back unconscious, like I said." There was a flurry of discussion in Korean between the old man named Chiun and the young wise guy.

"No!" Chiun said finally in English. "He is a man. He will walk."

"Walk where?" Barney asked belligerently.

"Tenth Avenue in midtown."

"What for?"

"We're supposed to keep you alive."

"On Tenth Avenue? I'd have a better chance of staying alive in the Klondike wearing a jockstrap."

"Breathe in the other direction," Remo said.

"Who sent you here?"

"Your fairy godfather. Get moving."

Barney bristled. "Look, you guys, I appreciate what you did for me back there, but I want to know where I'm going and why."

Remo sighed. "Let me knock him out," he said to Chiun.

"You are in no danger with us," Chiun explained. "However, our employer feels that others will attempt to do you harm. We are to protect you."

"So why do you have to protect me on Tenth Avenue? Why not just follow me home to Weehawken?"

"Because you've decided to murder somebody," Remo said, disgusted. "And I've got to ask Upstairs if you're allowed to. Complications. Always complications."

Chiun smiled proudly. "I knew he was an assassin."

"A fellow's got to earn a living," Barney said.

They turned left on 81st Street, where muffled music leaked from a cellar door. "Oh," Barney said excitedly. "I almost forgot about this place. A terrific after-hours club. Care to join me for a cocktail?"

He veered off. Remo collared him.

This upset Barney. Did they know that he might not make the trip back to Tenth Avenue alive without some liquid refreshment to quench his thirst? Did they know they might well be delivering a corpse to their employer? Did they want that?

"Walk," Remo said.

"If I fought you, you'd win, right?"

"Wouldn't be surprised," Remo said.

"If you knocked me out, would you carry me?"

"I suppose I'd have to," Remo said.

"Where on Tenth Avenue are we going?"

"Forty-fourth Street."

"That's too far. A cocktail, or I go unconscious." He offered his neck to Remo.

Just then, a gang of eight Puerto Rican street toughs approached them. One of them was picking his teeth with a stiletto. They circled the three strangers in the neighborhood.

"Hey, man, you got any change?" the one with the stiletto asked Chiun, teasing the knife around his wrinkled throat.

"You are annoying me with that toy," Chiun said.

The eight of them laughed.

"Tell them to go suck a mango," Remo suggested to Chiun.

"How about this toy?" another asked, flicking out his stiletto with a pop. Six more pops punctuated the night. Eight blades flashed. The circle closed more tightly.

Barney moved into position, but Remo pulled him away. "He can take care of himself," he said.

"What do you say, old man?" the leader sneered. "Got any last words?"

"Yes," Chiun said. "Twice this night I have been inconvenienced by groups of hooligans with knives. It is getting to be impossible to walk these streets, and I plan to complain about it. I suggest you stop bothering innocent pedestrians and go home. Also, it is disrespectful to call me old."

The leader poised his stiletto at Chiun's throat. On the other side, another gang member crept up behind Chiun, prepared to slash at his back. "Those your last words, man?"

"Yes," Chiun said. And then he kicked behind him to relocate the manhood of the approaching man into the man's kidneys and the gang leader was thrusting his stiletto into thin air as he hurtled above the heads of his associates and came to rest around a telephone pole, which he encircled like a wreath halfway up the pole.

Two gang members fled immediately. The remaining four bashed their heads together with the perfect synchronization of a Busby Berkeley chorus line as Chiun whirled around them. Their skulls cracked and flattened on impact.

The man with relocated testicles rolled over once with a groan and then was silent. The man hugging the telephone pole slid bonelessly to the ground.

"Irritating," Chiun muttered, turning back to Remo and Daniels. "Egg juice. Knives. Name-calling. It is enough to cause indigestion. And you," he said, pointing menacingly toward Barney. "You will walk."

69

"Yes, sir. Nothing like a good walk to perk up the old circulation. That's what I always say. A good walk stills the nerves."

"And be silent."

Barney walked to Tenth Avenue as the dawn rose. In utter quiet.

Barney stuck a cigarette in his mouth as he entered the motel room. Remo crushed it into powder, so that Barney stood in the doorway holding a match to a one-inch filter. Then Remo reached into Barney's coat pocket and pulverized the rest of the pack.

"You could have just said you preferred I didn't smoke," Barney said. He looked around the room. "Real cozy. Where's my room?" Remo pointed.

Barney looked inside. "That's the bathroom."

"That's right. Go take a shower. You smell like a brewery."

"Okay, okay," Barney said. "You don't have to be rude about it."

"Be sure to lock the door," Chiun said. "One never knows what a pervert might try."

"Got a drink?"

"No," Remo said, glowering.

"Just asked, that's all. No reason to get touchy." Barney headed off toward the bathroom and turned on the shower.

Remo called Smith. "We've got Daniels here," he said.

"Whatever for?"

He told Smith about Gloria X and the Peaches of Mecca and Barney's assignment to kill Calder Raisin.

"It doesn't make any sense," Smith said.

70

"Glad you agree."

"What does any of this have to do with Hispania?" Smith wondered aloud.

"Probably nothing. He's probably just trying to pick up a few bucks. The question is, what do we do with this rum pot?"

"Hang on to him until I can put everything into the computer. Don't let him kill Raisin. What's Gloria X's address?"

Remo gave it to him as Smith punched the information into the computer console.

"And what's her real last name?"

"Raisin."

"What?"

"She's Raisin's wife. That's what she said."

Smith was silent for a long moment before he said, "She can't be."

"Why not? Interracial marriages and murder between spouses has never been big news."

"Because Calder Raisin's wife lives in Westchester with their two kids under another name, and they're all as black as Raisin is. He keeps their profile low for security reasons, but he spends the weekends there. That information is in every personal biographical printout on every computer in the country."

"Maybe he's got two wives," Remo offered.

"I'll check it out. How old is Gloria?"

"Mid-twenties. Southern accent. Fanatic about the upcoming black revolution."

"Good," Smith said, keying in the material. "I'll go through the SDS and black organizations lists. Anything else?"

Remo thought for a moment. "She talks a lot while screwing."

Smith's keyboard fell silent. "Is that everything?" he asked drily.

"I guess so." Remo heard the phone click off.

It just didn't make sense.

Smith read the printout on the video screen for the third time:

RAISIN, CALDER B.

B. 1925, BIRMINGHAM, ALA.
ATTENDANCE, MERIWETHER COLLEGE, 1 YR.
PRESENT OCC: DIRECTOR, UNION RA-CIAL JUSTICE (URGE)
FORMER OCC: ASST. DIR., RAY THE JUNKMAN, INC., NEW YORK CITY.
FORMER OCC (2): SANITATION PERSON-NEL, CITY OF NEW YORK
MARRIED 1968, LORRAINE RAISIN, FORM. DALWELL
CHILDREN (2) LAMONTE, B. 1969, MAR-TIN LUTHER, B. 1974.
NO PREV. MARRIAGE OR OFFSPRING
INCOME: $126,000
HEALTH: POOR

SUB (1) HEALTH

CANCER, COLON. TERMINAL
HOSP: ROOSEVELT, 8/79
      ROOSEVELT, 5/79
      ROOSEVELT, 3/79
      LENOX HILL, 12/78
      A.B. LOGAN, 9/78
      N.Y. UNIV. HOSP, 2/78

"Cancer," Smith said out loud. What reason would anyone have for assassinating a terminal cancer patient?

The obvious answer, that Gloria X and her Peaches of Mecca didn't know about Raisin's illness, was too remote for Smith to consider. Any organization, particularly a black organization, willing to hire an assassin would know enough about Raisin to know he wasn't going to live long. But then the Afro-Muslim Brotherhood wasn't an official organization. In fact, the first traces of the Afro-Muslim Brotherhood that the computer was able to pick up had appeared less than a year before. During the same month that Barney Daniels had been returned from Hispania to the United States.

Blaming the assassination of a civil rights leader on an ex-CIA agent might make some sense as part of some larger scheme. It could make the agency look even worse to the public than it already did.

But as part of what larger scheme? What could Hispania, a banana republic no larger than Rhode Island, with a gross national product so small that most of its inhabitants lived in jungle huts—what could Hispania do to America?

America could wipe it out with a sneeze.

And even if Hispania were connected to the Afro-Muslim Brotherhood in some way, how could Smith explain the Hispania envelope filled with plastic explosive—the envelope that was delivered to Barney? And the name on the envelope, Denise Daniels. Who was she? There had been 122 Denise Danielses on Smith's printout, and none of them were related in any way to Bernard C. Daniels with the exception of a third cousin of Barney's uncle who lived in Toronto. Smith would have to create a new code to tap into international personal biographical data banks. He would begin with Hispania. But it could take years to sift through the names of every person, living or dead, in the entire world.

None of it made sense. But the weirdest piece of the puzzle was right in New York City.

Gloria X.

Who was Gloria X?

"A political genius with the body of a goddess, that's who you are," rumbled General Robar Estomago as Gloria rose from between his legs. "Also you give the best head in Puerta del Rey," he added with a chuckle.

"The best in the world, Robar honey," she said, rubbing her jaw. "Taking me out of that whorehouse and setting me loose back in America were the smartest things you ever did. Now I'm all yours." She rearranged herself on the bed in Estomago's office at the end of the Hispanian Embassy building.

"No, my hot puff pastry, not all mine. You are Hispania's. When you complete this mission, El Presidente De Culo will erect a statue of you."

"Hope it's more erect than El Presidente," she giggled.

"Your plan is going well, I take it?"

"Perfectly. I told you the bomb in the envelope wouldn't work. Daniels is too smart to be bumped off so easily. This way, we get rid of him nice and legal, and crack this two-bit country apart while we're at it. This place'll be so torn up with riots and demonstrations that nobody will even see us coming."

"Boom," Estomago said, gesturing wildly. "El Presidente will love that. And so will our Russian sponsors."

"That's right, sweetie. And you're going to love this."

At that, Gloria X nestled her head against the belly of the Hispanian ambassador and began to prove herself again.

General Robar Salvatore Estomago, chief emeritus of the National Security Council of the Republic of Hispania, current ambassador to the United States, and recipient of the considerable personal favors of Gloria X, had come a long way from flipping Big Macs at the local McDonald's franchise in Puerta del Rey.

The short-order stint was a post he had held immediately prior to his appointment as head honcho of Hispania's secret police under El Presidente Cara De Culo.

He shifted his rotund lower belly to grant Gloria better access to his legendary tool which, were it not for its exemplary size, would be all but hidden from view by the porcine proportions of his torso.

Her head bobbed enthusiastically, her blonde hair spilling out over his swarthy skin like a golden cloud. All his life he had fancied gringo women, white as diamonds. And Gloria was white to the core. She embodied everything he had ever dreamed or feared about white women. Gloria was beautiful, cruel, deceitful, duplicitous, selfish, spoiled, and unaccustomed to any sort of work. She was also utterly contemptuous of her homeland, and sought to destroy America with more zeal than El Presidente and the Russian premier combined.

Estomago knew he'd found a treasure in Gloria the minute she walked down the ramp of the American ship onto the docks at Puerta del Rey, whistling as she stripped to the skin and started soliciting the dock workers.

She had come with a shipload of women, volunteers anxious to get out of American prisons, even if it meant a long rehabilitation work program in Hispania. But the work was top-secret and all the workers were fated for disposal and since Gloria was blonde and Estomago lusted for her, he saved her from the normal work details, and put her in an occupation more suited to her talents. He set her up in the biggest whorehouse in town, with instructions to report on every important American who visited the place.

It was a good move. Because of one American, a CIA agent who knew more than agents in Hispania were supposed to know, Estomago was now ambassador to the United States. Also because of that one American—Bernard C. Daniels—a grand scheme was now coming into play, a scheme devised by Gloria to disrupt the United States, upset the balance of power in the world, and to thrust Hispania to world power, just as surely as Estomago was thrusting now under the expert guidance of Gloria's tongue and lips.

"Ah yes," Estomago sighed, fanning himself with a framed photograph of El Presidente, which he kept by the bed. "You sure know your business."

"Destroying America is my business," she said curtly, wiping her mouth. "In spite of these black fools you have saddled me with."

"The Afro-Muslim Brotherhood is a good cover for us," Estomago said. "Besides, you were the one who thought of creating it in the first place."

"It'll serve its purpose," she said. "I'm sending Daniels out to bump off Calder Raisin. That ought to work the niggies into a rampage."

"And Daniels? Did he object?"

"That poor drunken thing? I told him I was Raisin's wife and that I was after the insurance money."

"An American will always believe in greed," Estomago said loftily.

## CHAPTER SEVEN

"Gone? What do you mean he's gone?"

Remo ran into the bathroom where Chiun stood on the toilet lid, peering out the open window. "A true assassin," Chiun said, glowing. "Nothing can deter him from his goal."

"I've got to get to Raisin," Remo said.

The leader of URGE stood on the front steps of Longworth Hospital. He was wearing a short white hospital gown tied by two bows in the back, revealing a pair of red and green striped shorts. Before him, a dozen demonstrators similarly attired sprawled across the expanse of marble steps reading comic books and passing marijuana joints. Ahead of them, television cameras recorded the proceedings.

"My fellow freedom fighters," Raisin intoned into the microphones in front of him. A breeze shimmied through the thin gown he was wearing, causing it to ripple at his knees.

"I stand before you today in the cause of justice."

77

He turned aside and hissed, "Sheeit, brother, it cold out here. Go get me my robe."

A white man whose hospital gown was adorned with buttons advocating peace, the abolition of nuclear power, the execution of the Shah of Iran, the expulsion of whites from South Africa, the elimination of noise from urban centers, and a very old one demanding the death of anyone over thirty years of age, shuffled into the hospital to get Raisin the robe.

"I urge you to join us here at Longworth Hospital to help us meet our demands for equality in the medical profession. I urge you to participate in our call to action. I urge you to answer that call with us. Because, fellow supporters of this nation's oppressed Block Mon, the URGE must be met."

He pointed his finger in the air and scowled ferociously at the cameras. "And I tell you now as I stand before you, that I have more than a dream. I tell you, with four hundred years of black servitude echoing these words through the ages: I'VE GOT THE URGE!"

The people on the steps stirred. A young couple groped each other. Several of the pot smokers lay snoring. A tall black man wearing mirrored sunglasses shook a tambourine in time to disco music playing on his trunk-sized portable radio. "And you know, all of you who seek to break the chains of inequality, that when you've got the urge, you've got to do your duty!"

Remo walked up to Raisin. He wore a hospital gown untied over black chino pants and a tee shirt. He offered Raisin his robe. "Someone's going to try to kill you soon," Remo whispered, his back to the cameras.

78

"Who you?"

"Never mind. Get back inside the hospital."

"Fellow freedom fighters," Raisin shouted into the microphones. "I have just been informed that an attempt is being made on my life."

The groping couple squeezed closer together, their lips parted in ecstasy. The tambourine player rolled off to sleep.

"Would you shut up?" Remo said.

"And I say to you. I do not fear death from the hands of an assassin."

"Be quiet, will you? Just get inside."

"For what does a life signify without the full achievement of freedom for the Block Mon? I stand ready to die. And every Block Mon, woman and child stands ready to die in the cause of freedom."

Raisin's chest puffed out. His chin jutted forward. One shoulder rose higher than the other and he planted one foot out in front of him as though he were a mold for a bronze statue. "Freedom now," he shouted.

The young couple began to copulate and rolled into the range of the cameras. "Cut!" somebody yelled from behind the TV equipment. "Get those two screwers out of here, will you?"

As the couple was being rolled out of sight, Remo once again requested that the director of URGE return to his hospital bed where he could be protected while Remo searched out his assassin.

"Thank you, boy, but nobody going to kill me 'fore the Lord do hisself. Besides, they all these TV cameras around. Ain't nobody going to do nothing serious on TV." He patted Remo on the shoulder. "You just go about your business. I'll get inside quick as I can. And thanks for the tip. It make a good speech. Freedom now!" he repeated into the cameras, which had been turned on again, the screwers having been removed.

Remo walked through the sparse crowd. No sign of Daniels. If Barney hadn't come directly to Calder Raisin, Remo reasoned, he must have gone back to see Gloria X for instructions. He would be back in Harlem.

Barney eased himself out of the taxi, his head pounding. Eight o'clock in the morning, and not one drink since before dawn.

Some protectors, Barney thought, remembering Remo and Chiun. They might be able to fight, but nobody who would refuse a drop of tequila to a thirsty man was any friend of his.

He pounded on the door to Gloria X's house. The Grand Vizier Malcolm opened it at once. Obeying orders, Malcolm stepped aside to allow Barney to race to the bar in the living room.

Perched on top of the bar was a silver hip flask of tequila with a note attached. It read: "I'm yours whenever you want me."

He unscrewed the cap and sniffed. The welcome aroma of fine tequila filled his nostrils and coursed down his throat, beckoning for more. "Oh, baby, do I want you," he said to the flask.

He let the glory gallop down his throat. Then he filled it up again after locating the tequila bottle.

"Dat's all, whitey," the Grand Vizier said, striding across the white room. "You coming with me now."

"Hold it, Baby Huey," Barney said. "I am to be admitted to the bar anytime I feel like it. Your massa told me."

The Grand Vizier lifted Barney over his head and

carried him aloft out the door and into a black automobile, where two Peaches of Mecca snorted awake. Barney would have slugged it out with all of them were it not for the fact that he still held the cap to the hip flask in one hand and had to screw it back on so that the tequila in the flask would not be spilled.

As soon as he was tossed into the car, Barney was enveloped in a rough wool burnoose and handcuffed.

"I realize I ought to be getting used to this, but do you mind telling me where we're going?" he asked.

"We going to the Mosque," one of the Peaches said reverently. "You keep that hood over your face when we go in, else you get killed."

The Afro-Muslim Brotherhood mosque, about twenty minutes from Gloria X's, was identifiable by a hand painted sign on unvarnished plankboard nailed over another sign reading: *Condemned Building. Do not enter.*

"Open, doors of the faithful," the two Peaches cried in unison. The doors swung open heavily. Awfully heavily, Barney noted, for a condemned building that looked as though it would crumble to dust at a touch. And the doors were new. Fragments of steel shavings still clung to the hinges.

Barney was led through a maze of hallways, stairwells, past closed doors and giant empty rooms. The building had evidently been some kind of public building at one time, abandoned after Harlem ceased to be a quiet suburban retreat for middle-class white professionals and became the black Harlem it was today.

Barney could tell by the sound of his feet against the flooring that he was walking on a steel base. He bumped a wall with his elbow. Again steel. There were no windows.

The mosque was as well fortified as Gloria X's house.

Flanked by his two bodyguards, Barney ground to a halt in front of an enormous hall where a speaker, wrapped in purple swaths of silk, entreated his audience.

"Who keep you down?"

The answer was a soft grumble from five hundred black throats: "Whitey."

"Who kill our kids in these dirty slums?"

"Whitey."

"Who rob you, rape you, steal your bread?"

"Whitey."

"Who plan to wipe out the black man?"

"Whitey."

The speaker roared on, his voice rising above women in purple scarves on the left side of the old amphitheater, and above the dark, clean-shaven heads of the black-suited men on the right.

The speaker yelled. He pleaded. He cried out in the tradition of the black preacher. The temperature inside the old theater rose with the speaker's volume, manufacturing waves of perspiration. It flowed from black foreheads, black backs, black cheeks. It swamped brown armpits. It trickled down tan legs and tan spines. Yet no one moved. They sat rigid as soldiers, a theater full of zombies. Their only sign of life was the movement of their mouths as they murmured "Whitey."

"Whitey own this world," the speaker continued, "and he hate you. He hate your pure blackness which remind him of his own ugly white skin.

"He hate your strength and your courage and your wisdom. That why he want to kill you."

He paused a moment and smiled, a gold-toothed smile, a smile that cost him $4,275, from a white dentist in the Bronx, a smile he had bought while preaching for the Pentacostalist Gospelry Church. And that had paid well. But this paid unbelievably. That white woman with the blonde hair sure knew how to get his oratory moving.

"Whitey want to kill you, but we not gonna let him. You know why?" The hall was tomb-silent. "Because we gonna kill him, dat's why. We gonna end this blue-eyed tyranny over our lives.

"What we gonna do?" he asked. After a dramatic pause, he answered himself in a stage whisper. "We gonna kill, kill, kill." And then to the audience: "What we gonna do?"

Men stood to scream, released at last from the torture of their hot wooden seats. Women clapped their hands joyously. They all screamed, "Kill, kill, kill!"

"What ya gonna do?" the speaker asked again.
"Kill, kill, kill!"
"Say it again, children!"
*"Kill, kill, kill!"*
"Let Whitey hear you tell it."
*"Kill, kill, kill!"*

"Nice to see a community working together," Barney said to the two men at his sides. He reached for his hip flask, forgetting that his hands were cuffed together. As he was entangling himself in the folds of his burnoose, a figure veiled thickly in white tulle passed by, leaving a scent of lilacs in her wake. The Peaches of Mecca followed her, pressing Barney between them.

She led them through another maze, up a concrete stairway, down a long hall, through an empty room, and up another staircase. The stairs ended at yet another stairwell, this one a spiral of precision-made structural steel.

"You may wait here, gentlemen," the woman said, her voice dripping with plantation charm. The two Peaches nodded impassively. One of them handed her the key to Barney's handcuffs.

He followed her into an apartment of sparkling white, identical to her house in every detail except for a world map on a wall behind a white desk. There she removed her voluminous veil and white cloak. As Barney watched, she pulled off her opera-length white gloves. She untied a white rope belt around her waist. The dress she wore draped over one of her creamy shoulders and cascaded in Grecian folds to the floor, clinging to her curves all the way down. Smiling into Barney's hungry eyes, she pulled at the clasp over her shoulder with her manicured nails and let the dress fall to her feet.

She was naked beneath. Slowly, she stretched her arms over her head so that her breasts lifted beguilingly. Then she brought her hands down over the length of her body, caressing herself, her hips undulating, as Barney looked on, his hands chained together. It was a strangely familiar motion. Had he seen it before?

"I'm going to free your bonds now, Mr. Daniels," she purred.

"Allah be praised," Barney said. He was sweating hard in his woolen monk's robe.

She pressed one of her breasts into Barney's mouth as she unlocked the handcuffs. He did not take his lips from her as his hands searched out and found the treasure they were looking for. Then he moved his mouth away from her shiny wet nipple and wrapped it over the opening of the hip flask he had raised and was now emptying into his gullet. "Great stuff," he said appreciatively.

Gloria pulled him over to the bed and sated herself on him. As she came, screaming, Barney's hand fumbled over the surface of the nightstand for the bottle of tequila she had waiting for him. He took a swig, careful not to knock the bottle on Gloria's still thrashing head.

"That was great," she said dreamily.

"Best tequila I've ever had," Barney said.

"You don't care for me at all, do you?" Her voice grew suddenly cold.

Barney shrugged. "As much as I care for anything else," he said.

It was the truth. He would sit on Gloria's white Disneyland bed and fake love with her and let her dictate the part he would play in her little drama, because he had no other part to play. Barney's part had been left in Puerta del Rey a lifetime or two ago, and what he had now was his tequila, and nothing more.

He had gotten into this on a drunken whim and now he was a prisoner as sure as if he were in jail. It was a plush prison, to be sure, but a prison nonetheless, and Barney knew the sentence would be death, either from Gloria X and her trained seals or from the two men who had tried to help him.

He didn't want help. He didn't care if his death came soon or late. It was already long overdue. He had already been dead for a long, long time.

So why was he thinking about Puerta del Rey again? There was no answer to that most elementary question, the only question he ever asked: What happened? What happened? He forced his mind away from it. He made himself concentrate on the satin cushions around him on the bed, and on the tequila, and the tequila and the tequila.

And before the bottle was empty, the world was good and fine with Bernard C. Daniels.

Then he smelled the lilac perfume. "Wake up," Gloria said, shaking him. "It's night."

"Hell of a time to wake up."

"It's time."

"Time for what?"

"For killing Calder Raisin." She smiled, her lips stretched tight across her teeth. Blurred through Barney's drunken vision, her face appeared to him like a grinning death's head skull through a misty fog. "I had you moved here when I heard you'd made contact with your CIA friends."

"Don't have friends in the CIA," he said, his mouth still fuzzy.

"Those two on the corner. My men saw you. But now they don't know where you are, so they won't be able to help you, poor baby. You're going to have to kill poor Calder all by yourself." She patted his cheek. "Get up now. You have an appointment with Mr. Raisin at the Battery."

"What if I don't kill him?" Barney asked.

"Then you don't get the thousand dollars, darling," she said sweetly. "And you lose your life very painfully in the process. You know what 'painfully' means, don't you? Do you remember the pain, Mr. Daniels, or has the scar on your stomach healed completely?"

He leaped at her. "What do you know?" he demanded. "Tell me!" But her bodyguards were in the room, and pulled him away from the woman as she shrieked laughter as cold and shrill as the wail of a banshee.

\* \* \*

86

There were no television cameras on the pier, as the two black reporters dressed in neat black suits had promised Calder Riaisin back at the hospital. Nor were there any microphones on the creaking boards of the deserted place where a group of demonstrators was supposed to be waiting for him.

As soon as the limousine filled with overly friendly reporters deposited Raisin at the pier and sped away into the darkness, he knew the black reporters were fakes and he had been brought to this isolated spot to be killed.

Calder Raisin shook his head. He had been warned.

A man was waiting for him, sitting on the planks, his back resting against a barnacle-encrusted dock support.

Only one man, thought Calder Raisin. But then it would only take one man to kill him. It was his own fault, Raisin reprimanded himself, for not listening to the young white man at the hospital rally. Well, there wasn't much he could do now. He would just try to get it over with as fast as he could.

"What you want?" Raisin asked, turning up the collar of his bathrobe to protect himself from the wind. He shifted his weight from one hospital slipper to another to fend off the chilly wind. His hands were stuffed deep inside the pockets of the robe from which, at the bottom, a half-inch of hospital gown protruded.

"I said, what you want," Raisin repeated. "Look, you gonna kill me or what?"

Barney looked up, first at Raisin, and then off over the glistening black water.

"See here. I didn't come all this way to stare at New York Harbor with you. Now, you gonna 'sassinate me, or I going to walk away?"

Barney looked out over the water. It reminded him of a giant inkwell. A place where all the words of his life could be obliterated in an instant. Words like honor. Decency. Love. Words he had lived by once, when he had had a reason for living. One jump, and he could be as dead and as meaningless as those words. The water would swallow him up, and the remains of Barney Daniels would disappear into it. The water. The cold, bleak, unforgiving, welcome water.

"Snap to, boy," Raisin said, bending over to slap Barney on the shoulder. "It's cold out here. You gonna freeze."

Barney stared out over the water.

Raisin's voice softened. "Hey, want to grab a cup of coffee somewheres?" the portly black man asked.

But Barney only stared.

Raisin picked up his red terrycloth slipper and bounced it on Barney's head. "Look alive, man," he shouted. "What is this stupidness? I get hauled out here in the middle of nowheres, getting the crap scared out of me 'cause I thinking you gonna kill me, and now you ain't about to do nothing. You on junk, boy?"

Barney didn't answer.

"You wasting my time. I got a sick-in demonstration going, so if you ain't going to rub me out, I better get back to it 'fore I die of the cold."

Barney offered Raisin his flask. "Have a drink," he said. "It'll warm you."

Raisin drank. "Man, what is that shit? Tastes like poison."

"Tequila," Barney said, regaining possession of the silver container. "But it could have been poisoned."

"Sure as hell tasted like it."

88

Ignoring the crass comment, Barney lifted the flask to his lips and let the liquid pour down his throat. "I could have poisoned you, you know," he said.

Raisin shrugged.

"Your wife wants me to kill you."

"Lorraine? What she want to do that for? Who gonna pay the bills on that split-level money-eater in Whiteyville?"

"Not Lorraine. Gloria. Your wife. The blonde."

"My wife ain't no blonde," Raisin protested. "Leastways she wasn't four days ago. Lorraine look mighty silly a blonde. I gonna slap her silly if she done dyed her hair. Blonde. Hmmph."

"Gloria," Barney said, louder.

"I don't know no Gloria, stupid white ignoramus. You done come down here to kill the wrong man. Good thing you spaced out."

"Her name is Gloria, I tell you," Barney shouted, "and she's paying me a thousand dollars to kill you."

Raisin hopped up and down, his jaw thrust forward. "Well, then, you do that, smartass. You just try and kill me." He put up his fists. "Weirdo white junkie."

"Oh, get lost," Barney said.

"I ain't leaving till you 'pologize for calling my wife a white woman."

"I won't apologize. Go."

"I ain't going."

"Then you'll have to die here on the pier, because the drink I gave you was poisoned." Barney stood up to leave.

"Woah," Raisin said, restraining Barney with a shaky black arm. "You lying. Speaking falsehoods. You lying, ain't you?"

89

Barney ambled toward the end of the pier and sat down, his legs dangling off the edge. The water. The black, forgetful water.

"Wait, man," Raisin said, running to him and grabbing his arm.

"That's my drinking arm," Barney said. He yanked it free and took a long swallow from his flask.

"You ain't put nothing in that drink you give me, did you? I mean, you drank it yourself. Ain't nothing in it, right? Did she pay you in advance, or is she waiting for you to finish me off?"

Daniels pondered a moment, peered into the desperate eyes of a fellow human being, contemplated the obligation of all mankind to be responsible for all mankind, the true meaning of brotherhood, mercy and love and finally decided that if he were to relieve Raisin's doubts it might be whole seconds before he could get back to his flask of tequila.

"Yes," Barney said with finality. "It was poisoned."

"Oh, Lordie Lord!" Raisin's hands clutched around his throat.

"And I'm going to sit right here and die with you," Barney said, thumping on the rotted wood of the pier. "The perfect murder-suicide."

Calder Raisin ran off into the night, up the length of the pier and deep into the shadows behind. But it was only a matter of seconds after Raisin scurried away until Barney heard a thud, and then the whooshing of air a man makes when his lungs are collapsing, and then a small moan. And another thud.

Then they were on him, around him, behind him, hundreds of them, it seemed.

Then Barney felt the sharp, searing pain, acid

pain, oh, beautiful, numbing, terrible, shaking pain.

Frantic footsteps tore away into the blackness. Barney felt beneath his shoulder blades for the wounds. Just a little oozing dampness from all three cuts. He had not lost much blood, but oh God, the pain. Barney leaned against a dock support, fought to bring air into his lungs, then staggered up the ramp like a drunk.

And then he thought he saw her again. Once again, as though she had never gone.

"Denise," he whispered. Her face was in front of him again and she was smiling and the smell of her was on him, warm and giving and forever, before she began to fade again, into the black sea and the fetid air of the harbor.

"Denise," he called into the cold wind. But she was gone. Again.

He fell. And then there was blackness, the blackness for which he was grateful after an endless lifetime of waiting.

# CHAPTER EIGHT

When Gloria X entered her house in East Harlem, Malcolm was not at the door to greet her. He was inside, at the base of the stairwell, his neck broken so that his head joined his massive body at a perfect right angle. Surrounding him and leading up the stairs were the corpses of six other Peaches of Mecca, their arms and legs splayed over the steps like broken dolls, their blue-edged knives glinting beside them.

Silently, she pulled a small revolver out of her purse and followed the trail of bodies up to her bedroom.

The door was open. She listened. Nothing. Slowly she stepped inside, her revolver steady in her outstretched hand, positioned low for firing.

There was no one in the room. She circled it once, careful to keep one eye on the doorway. No one. Not a sound.

Then he came through the window as suddenly as a breeze, and the gun left her hand and soared out of reach as Remo clasped her wrists together behind her with one hand and held her throat with the other.

"Where is he," he said quietly. "I haven't got much time."

She closed her eyes with a shudder. Remo squeezed. "Barney Daniels," he said, pressing the veins in her neck. "I know you've sent him out to kill Calder Raisin. Where are they?"

"I don't know who you're talking about," she said levelly. "I never heard of him. And I don't know anything about Cald—"

Remo's grip tightened until her eyes bulged. "You have three seconds," he said. Her tongue began to ease out of her mouth, encircled by white foam.

"One," Remo said. "If you faint first, I'll kill you anyway. "Two."

"At the pier," she croaked. Remo softened the pressure slightly. "The abandoned pier at Battery Park, near the Staten Island Ferry."

92

"Good girl." Remo took his hand away and threw her into a corner of the room as if he were tossing a wet washrag.

She spun around on her knees. Crouched on all fours, she raised her head and laughed like a mad dog, her hate-filled eyes glistening. "You'll be too late," she spat, her voice still gravelly. "Raisin's dead by now. And so's your friend."

"Then I'll be back," Remo said coldly.

He found Raisin first, crumpled in a heap with his head bashed into bloody mush. On the pier, the silhouette of Daniels's body, doubled over, stood out starkly against the horizon.

There was an odd smell about him as Remo rolled him over to look at the knife wounds in his back. A familiar smell, but faint in the musky night air of the waterfront.

Remo held two fingers to Barney's temple. The weakest trace of a pulse remained.

Then he spotted the knife. Still holding Barney, he picked it up. Toward the base of the blade a blue stain shone in the moonlight. Remo lifted it near his face.

Curare. That was the blue on the knives of the well-dressed black men around Gloria's house. This was the scent they carried.

The pulse was fading fast. Too late for a doctor. Too late for anything now. "Looks like your last binge, sweetheart," Remo said to the unconscious form in his arms. He picked up Barney's silver flask lying on its side a few feet away, and knew it didn't matter any more. "Have a drink, buddy."

He raised the flask carefully to Barney's parched lips. He would wait with him until the end came. He would wait, because he knew that one day it would be Remo lying alone on a pier or in a street or behind a building in some place where he would be a stranger, since their kind were always strangers. He would wait because when that day came, perhaps there would be someone—a casual passerby, maybe, or a drunken derelict who made his home nearby—who would hold him as he now held Barney Daniels, and who would offer him the warmth of human contact before he left his life as he had lived it. Alone.

Barney's lips accepted the last of the alcohol. He stirred. One hand moved slowly toward Remo's and clasped it weakly.

"Doc," Barney said, so softly that normal ears could not have heard it.

"Barney?" Remo asked, surprised at the restorative powers of the drink. "Wait here. I'll get a doctor."

"Listen," Barney said, his face contorted with the effort. Remo leaned closer. Barney whispered a telephone number.

Remo left him on the pier as he ran into Battery Park to reach a pay phone.

"Jackson," a man's bass voice answered.

Remo gave the man directions to the pier, then went back to Barney, whose breathing was so labored that, even in the chilly night, drops of sweat dotted his upper lip and forehead. "Hang on," Remo said. "Doc's coming."

"Thanks . . . friend," Barney said, the muscles in his neck straining.

As the gray Mercury skidded to a halt by the pier, Barney's head dropped backward and he slumped unconscious again in Remo's arms.

A tall black man, elegantly dressed, approached them with a stride faster than most men's at a full run. "I'm Doc Jackson," he said with authority. "Get him in the car."

"I don't think he's going to make it," Remo said.

"I don't care what you think," Doc answered, his lips tightened in grim determination as they sped away. Behind them, rolling to a stop at the pier, Remo could see the flashing red lights of police and emergency vehicles and the carry-all vans of New York's television stations.

# CHAPTER NINE

Robert Hansen Jackson was born on a little island off the Carolinas in 1917. His father ran the only hotel there. His mother was a seamstress.

"Your daddy can read, Robert. He's a man," his mother would say often. And then she would tell him about the Blessed Virgin and say the rosary and make him say it with her.

Robert Jackson would move his mouth and pray that the session would soon be over.

One day, his mother told him that the Spanish priest would leave the island because San Sendro was now an American possession. It had been for years, since what she called the big war over Cuba, but now they would be getting an American priest because San Sendro had belatedly become part of the Archdiocese of Charleston.

The island turned out with bright banners and cleanest dresses and shirts for the American priest.

Robert's father was to give the welcoming address. The mayor would present a silver bowl of newly picked fruit. The mayor's wife and the town's leading ladies, including Robert's mother because she was married to a man who could read, would escort the Americano priest to Maria de Dolores Church.

Everyone had a part in the welcome, even little Robert. He and seven other boys, four on each side, would push open the doors as the priest entered the church.

Father Francis X. Duffy seemed impressed with his greeting. That's what everyone said. He said it was the most welcome greeting he had ever seen.

Then Father Duffy, who had been born in Myrtle Beach, South Carolina, gave the island some Americanizing. He told them San Sendro was now part of the land of the free and the home of the brave. And he proved it by establishing another church, St. Augustine's, and made all the dark-skinned people go there.

That was when Robert discovered he was a Negro. Father Duffy told him so.

San Sendro had been wallowing for decades in Spanish decadence, unaware of the importance of racial purity. One of Father Duffy's earliest and most difficult tasks in setting this straight was to determine who was black and who was not.

In their backwardness, the people had failed to sustain the purity of their blood lines. But Father Duffy kept at it. Church registration dwindled, not only from the newly discovered Negroes but from whites, too. Still Father Duffy persevered. And by

96

the time of his death, a visitor couldn't tell the difference between San Sendro and Charleston.

He knew he had done right, even though some meddling foreign priests expressed surprise. The previous pastor, whom Father Duffy suspected of having Negro blood himself, cried when he saw his island again.

He cried before the altar, and he cried while saying mass. And he cried when he tried to tell Father Duffy that what he was doing was wrong. Father Duffy so lost his temper that he called Father Gonzalez a nigger.

Then, making an act of contrition, he apologized to Father Gonzalez the next day.

"You need not apologize to me," Father Gonzalez answered. "In this parish, in your world, if I had a choice, I would be nothing but a nigger. For I tell you, if your world should prevail, and if it were bound in heaven as it is on earth, in separation of people by the color of their skins, then I would dread the last judgment if I had lived my life in a white skin.

"You have done more than separate people. You have decided who can be rich and powerful and who must be poor. And I tell you, just as it is difficult for a rich man to enter heaven, so will it be for a white man in your parish. It would be easier for a camel to pass through the eye of a needle. I do not pray so much for the blacks here. I pray for the whites. And I pray most of all, and I weep, for you, Father Duffy."

The trouble with some priests, Father Duffy thought, is that they take things too literally. They might as well become Baptists if they weren't going to use their reason.

Robert Hansen Jackson used his reason. He never set foot in a Catholic church again. His mother, however, continued to pray the rosary and attend mass, even when St. Augustine's Church showed a leak in the roof. She sat beneath the dripping water in the church, calling it God's sweet rain, and the holiest water of all.

And when she died, she was buried in the new Negro cemetery, never having missed mass a day in her life. Robert Jackson left the island. He was fourteen.

He floated around the Charleston docks for a year, but breaking his back for survival was not his game. One night, by himself, he climbed into a window of a doctor's office where he knew a large supply of morphine was kept. He could sell it big in New Orleans, while the police would undoubtedly look for a black man traveling north.

He was caught. An elderly white man with a pistol interrupted the thrust of a bottle into Robert's brown paper bag. He did it with a bullet.

Then he moved Robert to a table, turned on the lights, and proceeded to remove the bullet.

"Why are you taking it out?" Robert asked. "If you leave it in, there'd be one less nigger to dirty up your world."

"If I don't take it out," said the doctor, "there'd be one more doctor who has violated the Hippocratic oath."

"That Greek guy, huh?"

"That Greek guy."

"Well, I've seen it all now," said Robert, who suddenly discovered he would live. "A white man who does what he says he believes in. Wowee. Oh boy. I gotta tell this to the folks." He made obscene noises.

"We're no worse than any other race," the doctor said evenly.

"And better than mine, right? You think you're better than me, don't you?"

"Not necessarily. But for the sake of what I know, I'll say yes."

"Thought you would," Robert sneered.

"You were stealing from me, not me from you."

Robert straightened up. "Okay. I'll buy that, Doc. But why was I stealing from you? Because you had what I wanted. Why did you have it? And not me? Because I'm black, that's why."

"I had morphine in my possession because I'm a doctor. You obviously wanted it to sell. Your body has no needle marks."

"Well, why ain't I a doctor?"

"Because you never went to school to become a doctor. And don't say ain't."

"Well, why didn't I get to school to be a doctor?"

"Because you never applied, I imagine."

"Bullshit. Schools stink. I never applied because I never had the money. And if I did have the money, I wouldn't spend it on any damn doctor's school because a black doctor is just as poor as a black lawyer or a black anything else."

"Lie still. You're opening the wound."

"I'm opening a lot more," Robert said. "Now, I'm the smartest, toughest guy I know. And I know I could be a better doctor than you. That is, if my skin was white."

"Is that so?" the doctor said, smiling so small a show of amusement that Robert had never felt more insulted, not even when some people called him "boy."

"Yes, that's so. You just give me one of your

99

fancy medical books and I'll show you. That green one, up there on the top shelf."

"Turn my back on you, son? With that scalpel you're hiding under your shirt?"

Robert glared.

"Give it back handle first. That's the right way."

Offering a scalpel the correct way was the first thing Robert Hansen Jackson learned about medicine. The second was that the green book contained a lot of words that didn't make sense. The third was that with a little bit of explanation they did.

The doctor was so impressed that he did not surrender Robert to the police. Robert was so grateful that he hid only one bottle of morphine in his trousers when he left, just enough for money to get to New York, where he expanded his drug distribution long enough for him to be the first Negro to graduate from the Manhattan School of Medicine; the first Negro to practice at the Manhattan General Hospital; the first Negro to have an operational procedure concerned with the suturing of blood vessels accepted nationally.

That he was simply "the first doctor" to have invented the process was hardly mentioned. By the time World War II blossomed into American participation, he was tired of being "the first Negro."

He didn't wait for the draft. He volunteered. Not because he cared which white nation won the war, but because it gave him an excellent, conscience-salving excuse to leave his wife and other people who were ashamed of being born black.

His perfect knowledge of Spanish, the language of his childhood, his knowledge of medicine, especially surgery, got him rank in the young OSS. And he stayed on, into the years of the cold war.

The color of his skin got him to South America

where he could blend in with other brilliant Negro surgeons, namely none. Doc Jackson didn't blend, least of all where there was an absence of medical brilliance of any variety, black or white.

He stood out as he had stood out all his life, as "the best damned man around."

For four months once, on a jungle assignment in Brazil designed to make contact with a primitive tribe and show them, as one of the chiefs put it, "the white man's medicine and let them know where favors come from," Doc was struck with a comparatively sensitive agent with an extraordinary ability to care about what happened to people, including himself.

Other than that, Bernard C. Daniels was sober, industrious, and conscientious, as well as reliably and thoroughly sneaky. He was white.

It was dislike at first sight. Then it became hatred. Then grudging tolerance, and finally the only friendship Doc Jackson ever had in his life.

When Daniels finally left military service, so did Jackson, leaving behind them scores of dead bodies of men who had interfered with their missions. Doc picked up a few routine and boring threads of his past, establishing a clinic in Harlem because he was tired, lest he become "the first Negro" again.

Daniels joined the CIA. Doc heard from him only once, in a letter brimming with happiness, announcing his impending marriage.

He did not hear from Daniels again, even though he had mailed him his phone number and address several times after reading about Barney's bizarre turnaround on the island of Hispania.

He had wanted to see Barney, to visit his house in Weehawken and force his friendship back on a man who needed a friend. But Jackson would not force

Barney to lean on him. He respected his own privacy too much to invade another's, especially that of a man as lonely and troubled as Barney Daniels. When Barney needed him, he would call.

And when that call came, from a stranger saying that Barney was dying from curare poisoning on an abandoned pier in the dead of night, Doc Jackson was ready.

# CHAPTER TEN

Barney's peaceful death was shattered suddenly by blinding lights and nausea. Throbbing nails in the skull. Pain pins in the chest. Breathing hard. So hard.

"Breathe, Barney, damn it, you drunken Irish son of a bitch." The voice was harsh. Two strong hands worked over him. His mouth tasted of salt. That was a curare depressant. Had he been slashed with curare? Where would anyone up here get curare? Was the past following him?

Auca. Inca. Maya. Jivaro. Who still existed? Who used curare? Agony behind his pupils. Both arms numb. No, not numb, Barney realized as he faded into semi-consciousness. His arms were strapped down. So were his legs.

Was he back? Was it the hut in the jungle again, the poker glowing in the fire at the center, the machete poised above him, his arms and legs tied with hemp? Or had he never left? Would it never end?

"Breathe, damn it."

The machete! It was coming down, slowly now, into his arm. He tried to focus.

Not a machete. A tube, a tube from above, sliding painlessly into his left arm.

Then he saw Doc Jackson's face, perspiring and mad, the high black cheekbones, the deepset dark eyes, the rising forehead and short kinky hair. A face without fat, just taut, hard skin, with thick lips now grown tight and hard and cursing. "Damn you, you fucker, breathe, I said."

Doc, Barney wondered. How did Doc find the hut in the middle of the jungle? He'd left long before. Did he come back, just to save him?

The hands worked on his chest as the tube in Barney's arm replaced the poisoned blood in his body with fresh.

"Barney," Doc's voice commanded. "Barney, make yourself breathe. Force it." He beat down hard on Barney's chest.

Barney opened his mouth to scream when the pain, like cymbals in a tunnel, banged through him to the tips of his fingers.

"Good," Doc said, relieved. "You know you're alive when you feel pain. That's the only way you know. Dumb bastard. Don't talk. Just keep breathing."

"Doc," Barney said.

"Shut up, you stupid fuck. Breathe hard."

"Doc. Denise is dead."

"I know that. This isn't Hispania. You're in Harlem. In my clinic."

"She's dead, Doc."

103

"Keep breathing."

Barney breathed. And Doc Jackson's face disappeared into the lights above and Barney smelled hospital smells and then it was the smell of the Puerta del Rey waterfront, like a sewer beneath the sun, fermenting.

"How can you be here?" Was Barney talking? Was Doc answering? Who was answering?

"Keep breathing."

It was Denise who was talking. Oh, what a beautiful sunny day. What bright colors the women beneath the window were wearing. Oh, how beautiful if you could forget the smell, which you did when you had been there long enough and didn't think about it.

"The whole country knows why you're here, Barney," she said in her pleasant sing-song way.

Barney leaned against the window sipping a cup of rich black coffee. His hair was touseled and he wore a pair of striped undershorts and a shoulder holster with a long-barrelled .38 police special.

He waited to look around, because he knew that when he did, his heart would jump and he would want to sing when he saw her again. He was so happy he could have blown his brains out.

He had stalled headquarters for three weeks to stay in Puerta del Rey after a routine assignment was finished. It had to do with shipping and the CIA had flooded the area, taking no pains to disguise its presence. El Presidente Caro De Culo, the dictator of record, had been served notice not to interfere with banana shipments.

De Culo had received the notice, responded favorably, and the surface network of the CIA left the island with as much ostentation as it had arrived.

Not Barney. He had concocted a tale about a fictitious group seeking to overthrow De Culo, and the CIA left him there for a report. When the report was completed, he was to leave.

The report story had kept him afloat in Hispania for three weeks now. Three beautiful, glorious weeks.

"The whole country knows what you're doing, Barney. You haven't bothered to keep it much of a secret."

Some people said Denise had a raspy voice, but they didn't really appreciate the soft timbre tones flowing from her exquisite throat. They didn't know Denise.

Early on the regular assignment, Barney had been detailed to escort the vice-president of a large American fruit-shipping firm to a plush brothel and see that he returned with most of his money. More important, he had been told, was to see that the executive didn't get carried away with the little leather whip he liked to use. Mainly, it had been an assignment to smooth over whatever wrath the executive's perversions incurred.

It was not a pleasant assignment. But it was not a pleasant business. And the executive was a major figure in the banana triangle. So Barney had brought him to the house, had whispered a word of caution in the right places and the right girl followed the executive up a red carpeted stairway.

And then, for the first time, he had heard Denise's voice. "Don't you want someone?"

She was beautiful, breathtakingly beautiful, even though she dressed herself plainly, almost as though to hide her ripe, shapely body. And her face. Unadorned by makeup or jewelry, it possessed all of the finest features of every race on earth, blended together in unobtrusive perfection.

Her eyes were faintly almond shaped, colored light gray with sparks of blue and brown. Her skin was golden, slightly darker than Arabia, but lighter than Africa. It hinted of sunlight and moonlight at the same time, of Europe and the Orient. There was Indian in her, too, apparent by her prominent, strong bones and shapely lips, red and full and curving playfully at the corners.

She repeated her question, almost taunting. "Don't you want someone?"

Barney looked at her, let his gaze rise from her neat red leather shoes, up the bare legs, across the simple knit dress, and met her eyes. He smiled. "No, nothing. I'm here on business."

"What is your business?" she asked.

"Looking out after perverts, like the one upstairs."

"Yes, we know him. There is no worry. The girl can take care of herself. She is very well paid. There is no need for you to wait here, disturbing the other guests."

"I'm not leaving without him."

"I could have you thrown out. But I know you people would come back. Everyone knows your organization is here in numbers. Why don't you take one of the rooms upstairs?"

"I don't want one of the rooms upstairs."

Her smile of gentle condescension did something to Barney's gut. "Well, agent whoever-you-are, there really isn't too much I can do to stop you from standing here in the middle of the reception room and annoying the guests. Would you care for something to drink while you're ruining my business?"

Barney shrugged his shoulders uncomfortably. The other island girls he had known were different—giggling, pretty birds who teased and played and fluttered away. This one had a strength that unnerved him. It filled the room. It commanded.

"The bar is behind the staircase."

"I'll have coffee. Where's the kitchen?"

"I'll make it. Come with me."

They walked through a door into the rear of the building. Two uniformed maids playing cards suddenly jumped from their chairs and erupted in a geyser of excited and nervous Spanish.

"They're not used to seeing me here," Denise said. Neither was the cook who spilled hot soup on himself or a busboy who almost dropped a tray.

"Leave us alone," she said quietly, and the kitchen became vacant in an instant.

"I hate agents, policemen, assassins, extortionists, soldiers, and pimps," she said. She made the coffee from fresh ground beans in a copper pot.

Barney sat on a cutting board, dangling his legs, feeling his butt getting moist from recently butchered meat. He didn't care. He was watching Denise. For some reason, the sight of this woman making coffee was more thrilling to Barney than a forty-girl chorus line of nude beauties.

"You know, I don't find you at all attractive," she said.

"You don't appeal to me either."

Then they laughed. Then she served the coffee.

They talked a lot that night, Denise about the financial problems of payoffs, the difficulty she had in selecting bed partners, Barney about the boredom of his business, only kept interesting by its stakes, his success with women which somehow was never success, and the state of Hispania which neither of them cared very much about.

With the dawn, Barney left to escort the executive to a hotel and then a conference. They walked through streets of almost naked children. "One drop of nigger blood," the executive said, "and it destroys a race."

"I guess they become perverts," Barney said. He could see the executive contemplating a complaint to his superiors.

He returned to the whorehouse and Denise Saravena for three beautiful weeks.

One night, she said: "Barney, I want your baby. I could have it if I wanted without telling you. But I want you to know when we make love that I'm trying to conceive your child."

Barney didn't know why he couldn't speak. He tried to say something, anything, but all he could do was cry, and tell her that he could never be a father to her baby because he wasn't going to be around much longer. He wanted their baby to have a father.

Then Barney said that they were going to get married very soon because he did not want to do it without marriage anymore.

She laughed and told him he was romantic and foolish and lovely, but no, marriage was impractical.

Barney told her she was right, it would be highly impractical, and that they wouldn't make love any more until they were married.

Denise pretended to think this was very funny, that he sounded like a young girl waiting for a ring. That night she tried to seduce him as a game. It did not work. The next day they knelt before a priest in a small church near the American embassy and became husband and wife.

So he found himself, standing near a window on a bright morning, dressed in shorts and a shoulder holster, listening to the magnificent words of his complaining wife and loving every minute of it.

"They all know we're married, Barney. Everyone does. Sooner or later, even the CIA will find out."

Barney had savored the pleasure of gazing upon Mrs. Denise Daniels long enough that day. With a firm pirouette, he wheeled to embrace his wife, and, still holding his coffee, kissed her. Morning mouths and all, it was wonderful.

"Darling," she said, escaping long enough from his lips to talk, "I know this country. The moment you are without your country's protection, President De Culo and his gang will close on you. Darling, listen to me," she urged as he waved her worries aside like so many annoying flies. "He permitted your interference with the banana shipments only because he had no choice. This regime does not wish to be under American influence. De Culo rose to power from nothing, by offering money and food to his army."

"American money."

Denise shook her head. "For one so intelligent, my darling, sometimes you look no further than your own CIA does. The money De Culo uses now for his army is American money. Some of it."

Barney screwed up his face. "What are you talking about?"

"Some of the money is American," she repeated quietly. "Not all. What the United States cannot understand is that no population on earth outside of the American people require so much money for minimal subsistence. What you Americans call 'poor' is colossal wealth for us, and for every other people in the world. De Culo's money from the American government is a far greater amount than what is needed for the maintenance of his troops, and certainly more than necessary for De Culo's civil programs, since he gives nothing to the people to keep them from starving. All the money goes to the army. And there is more, much more."

"Like what?"

"Ammunition. Arms. Guns, grenades, food supplies. They are all stored underground, deep in the jungle. I know these things, Barney. My girls tell me. They are offered many presents in the course of a drunken evening with De Culo's swaggering officers, most of whom were starving and ragged as the rest of us before De Culo's mysterious appearance with enough money to organize an army and take over the government."

"We don't give arms to Hispania."

"No, you do not. You give money. De Culo buys the arms with American money. His general, Robar Estomago, makes the arrangements with the Russians."

"But there aren't any Russian installations here," Barney said stupidly. "No treaties, no pacts . . ."

Denise smiled and shook her head. "No, there are no official agreements with the Russians," she said sadly. "De Culo could not get the American money if there were. Hispania is too small and poor a country to be considered dangerous by the powerful United States. And so your CIA never looked for the Russian installation. And never saw the Russian guns. They have been well hidden. Your people wanted only to see the banana shipments, and so you saw bananas only."

"Jesus," Barney whispered. "I suppose De Culo's original money to start his army came from the Russians."

"Of course. And your government, which views Hispania as harmless and impoverished, viewed what they saw of De Culo's ragged little army, without uniforms and made up of the village poor, as a

110

feeble attempt at pride. They did not see the guns. They did not even look at a map."

She walked over to a battered cypress wood chest in the corner of the room and took from it a world map, its creases worn to holes from folding and refolding. She opened it flat on the table in front of Barney. On the map was drawn a network of fine red lines originating from Moscow and fanning out into the Middle East, Europe, Asia and South America, with a separate series of blue lines to Cuba. From Cuba, other blue lines emanated toward Puerta del Rey.

Barney sucked in his breath as he traced each line from Moscow to known Russian military installations around the globe. Although there were no codes on the map, there could be no mistaking the meaning of the lines. Broken red lines to France and Italy indicated peace treaties and possible allies in the event of full-scale nuclear war. Broken blue lines leading to strategically advantageous areas in the Middle East had to mean possible installations, or partially completed installations, in countries where the Russian army could seize the government by force when it decided to. Iran was a broken blue line. So was Afganistan. And so was Hispania.

But the most prominent line on the map was a hand drawn wobbling, drunken line orignating with a small ink blob on an uninhabited jungle border of Hispania, no more than three hours on foot from the spot where Barney and Denise were sitting at that very moment, and leading directly on a straight course over Cuba to Washington, D.C.

"I took this from one of the girls here," Denise said. "General Estomago's favorite. It had fallen under the bed. I found it after they had both left the room. The next day, one of Estomago's men came

111

around to ask if I had found a map outlining potential banana routes. Estomago must have thought I was stupid. Hispania has no reason to ship bananas to Cuba."

"This is a military map," Barney said. "Some of this information is so classified that the CIA doesn't even have it on file yet."

Denise nodded. "Yes, that line to Hispania is new. And so is that line from Hispania to Washington."

"You know what it means?" Barney said.

"Yes. It means that the Russians have waited for the right time and now have built a military installation on Hispania. A nuclear installation which they will unveil at the right moment and use to intimidate the United States. El presidente De Culo and General Estomago have been working on this for two years. Everybody knows about it."

Barney fingered the old map. "If everybody on this island knows about the Russian installation, why hasn't any word leaked out by now?"

Denise sighed. "You still do not understand," she said. "Hispania is a poor country. We do not care whether the Russians control our bananas or the Americans control our bananas. Whoever is on the dicator's throne at the moment will see to it that we do not get money for our bananas anyway, no matter what country he is allied with. We do not care about politics, because we are hungry. De Culo is a wicked man, but every dictator who has come to govern Hispania has been a wicked man. He is no more wicked than the rest. And in his army he feeds many of the young men of our villages. These are men whose families would starve, were it not for the scraps of American and Russian food supplies which they are able to steal and bring home to their

112

people. It is the only way we live. No, we will not talk about the Russian installation. Starvation of our entire country is too high a price to pay for one conversation with a drunken American ambassador."

"You said Estomago has a favorite girl here," Barney said. "Who is she?"

"She is a strange one. An American. I do not trust her."

"Why'd you take her on?"

"Estomago told me that I was to give her shelter and employment to customers of his choosing. She is not a regular working girl here. She is only for Estomago. And for others whom he selects."

"Like who?"

"The most prominent of your CIA men, usually. At first I thought she was a CIA agent herself, but I do not believe that is so. Her hatred for America is very deep. She slashed a young American visitor with a knife once."

"An agent?"

"No. Fortunately, he was a runaway soldier from the American army, so I was able to cover up the incident. But the girl is vicious. I dismissed her after the stabbing, but Estomago insisted that I take her back. He said he would close my house if I didn't. So she remains."

"I want to talk to her," Barney said, rushing to throw on a shirt and a pair of pants. "I want to see her right now."

"Be careful, darling," Denise warned. "She is Estomago's woman. And you are already being watched here, since you are the last American agent on the island. If she suspects that you know anything, Estomago will kill you."

"Tell her I'm on my last fling before heading home to the bad old USA."

"But she must know that we're married."

"That's perfect. Say you married me to get a passport out of this stinkhole, and you'll be leaving with me, just as soon as I have my fill of young poontang."

Denise led him upstairs to the girl's room. The door was closed.

"She is very private," she said. "This one never chats with the other girls or even dines with us. Always alone."

She rapped sharply on the door. After a few minutes, it was opened by a young, platinum-haired, thin-faced girl dressed all in white, her thin lips stretched taut against her teeth to resemble a skull.

"Yes," she drawled sullenly, the hint of the American South drawing out her word.

"I have a visitor for you," Denise said crisply. The girl turned her back on them and walked wordlessly toward the bed, unbuttoning her blouse.

Denise closed the door behind her as she left. "What's your name?" Barney asked, still standing inside the door, his hands in his pockets.

"Gloria," the girl said with a bored half yawn. "Come on. Get this over with."

"Gloria what?"

"Sweeney," the blonde said. "You come here to talk or screw?"

# CHAPTER ELEVEN

Barney Daniels's arm jerked upward with such force that it shredded the gauze wrapping which held it to the I.V. board bolted to the side of the bed.

The lone nurse monitoring the small section of the clinic rushed over. She pressed a button over the bed that rang a bell in Dr. Jackson's office.

"It's Barney," Jackson said to Remo as he took off at a run.

"Let me talk to him, Doc. If he's conscious, I want to talk to him."

"I don't want you aggravating my patient with any CIA bullshit," Jackson said as he burst through the double doors into Barney's room.

Thrashing under the hands of the nurse, his plastic bag of plasma jiggling precariously above him, Barney Daniels screamed.

It was an unconscious scream, wild and frightened. "The map," he shrieked, his voice breaking. "The map."

The night nurse watched the video monitors frantically as Barney's life signals peaked in jagged, uneven mountains. "There, there," she said uncertainly.

"Move aside," Jackson said as he approached the

bed. "Nurse, prepare two hundred thousand CC's of thorazine on the double."

He grabbed Barney by both flailing arms. "Settle down, Barney. It's Doc. I'm here."

"The map," Barney shrieked.

"Shut up, I said."

The nurse swung around to retie the gauze strips around Barney's arms as Doc's hands held them in place. Barney's hospital gown was drenched with sweat. His hair was matted with it, and it poured down his face in shiny streams.

"He's undergoing some kind of intense mental activity," the nurse said. "It's almost like a pentathol reaction."

"It's the curare," Jackson said as he accepted the needle from the nurse.

"No, Doc," Barney panted, his eyes rolling. "Listen to me. Listen . . . liss . . ." He forced his eyes to work.

"Let him talk," Remo said. "He could tell us something important."

Jackson looked over to Remo, his hypodermic poised in the air. "All right," he said. "Go ahead."

Remo touched Barney's arm. "The map, Barney."

"Map," he croaked.

"What map?"

"Gloria's map." He licked his cracked lips slowly. "Gloria's apartment. The mosque. Gloria in Hispania."

He smiled slowly, his eyes closing. "I remembered, Doc."

"You're better off forgetting all that, Barney," Jackson said quietly. "Whatever it was, it hasn't done you any good."

"I . . . remembered."

116

"Who is Gloria?" Remo asked. "What's her name?"

"Gloria . . ."

Jackson checked the monitor. Its lines were still peaking dangerously.

"Gloria who?"

"That's enough," Jackson said. "He's going to go into shock if you don't stop." He moved forward to press the needle into Barney's intravenous tube.

"Gloria . . ." Barney's chest heaved. His nose ran. Tears streamed from his eyes. "She was one of them, Doc. She helped kill Denise." He sobbed.

Jackson shot the last of the hypodermic into the tube. "It'll just take a second, Barney."

"Gloria who?" Remo demanded.

"Get out of here!" Jackson raged.

The nurse tugged at Remo's arm. He didn't move.

"Gloria . . ." The drug started to take effect. Barney's muscles relaxed. The monitor began to resume its normal wave pattern.

*Got to tell him*, a voice deep inside Barney prodded. *Tell Doc. Try. Try for Denise.*

"Sw— Sw—" Barney whispered. It was so hard to move his lips. So hard. Swimming so low, circling the bottom . . .

"Don't talk," Jackson said.

*Tell him for Denise. If you die, she deserves that much.*

"Sweeney," he gasped, hearing his own voice so far away that it sounded like an echo. Then he gathered together all the strength in his body and tried again.

"Sweeney," he shouted, so that Doc could hear him, so the world could hear, so that even Denise, or what was left of her in her unmarked grave, could hear.

117

"Sweeney!" he screamed again, as if by pronouncing the name he could expiate all the sins of the past and return to that time in his wife's kitchen when the sun was shining and the world was beautiful.

Then the thorazine took over, and he was back.

The installation had been carved out of mountain rock, lined with lights, floored with tile, heated by a vast steam system and camouflaged by the exterior of the mountain. The Russians had planted a new forest of trees in layers surrounding the entrance to cover the traces made while constructing the site. There was no road, however, since all of the equipment used for setting up the installation had been carefully hauled in by sea. It was a magnificent station, and undiscoverable.

"Mother of God," Barney whispered as he snapped a roll of film. He and Denise sat crouched in the jungle forest in front of the brilliantly illuminated installation where hundreds of Hispanian and Cuban soldiers worked.

"Now that you have seen it for yourself, we must leave quickly," Denise said. "It is very dangerous for us to remain here."

Barney looked at the sun licking through the trees above their heads. "It's hard to believe that this little island has the capability to blow up half the world," he said almost to himself.

"But of course these bombs never will have to be used," Denise said.

Barney nodded. He understood well what she meant. For years, America had maintained a rough equivalence with the Soviets in nuclear might and by this standoff had maintained an uneasy peace in the world. Each side knew that it faced almost total annihilation in the event of war. There had been an unspoken agreement between the superpowers not to try to expand their nuclear influence into areas where they had no real geographical or historical stake. The Russian attempt to move missiles into Cuba was a flagrant violation of this rule, and President Kennedy had backed the Russians down.

But times had changed. Kennedy had owned the military muscle to force the Russians to blink. Too many years of a White House that thought America could be guarded by good intentions had since reduced the country to a poor also-ran in the military might department, and there would be no forcing this installation out of Hispania just by words. It would stay there. And the balance of power in the world would forever have shifted. Missiles could be launched from Hispania anywhere in the United States or Caribbean and the Russians could say, "Who? Us? We didn't do it. Hispania did it on its own," and an American president, faced with an inadequate arsenal of his own, would have to decide: would he attack Russia in retaliation, knowing that the result would be the United States' destruction?

And so Russia would have conquered the world. Without a shot.

"Come," Denise said to Barney.

Taking him by the hand, she led him through the tangle of jungle rain forest toward their home in Puerta de Rey. Just as the two of them were approaching the outskirts of the lush, steaming jungle, silent but for the screams of exotic birds and chattering monkey noises from the heights of the tall banana trees, Barney whirled around, managing in one swift motion to knock Denise to the soft ground with one hand while drawing his .38 with the other.

"Don't fire," Denise hissed, clutching at his shirt. "One sound, and they will kill us without question."

Barney wasn't listening to her. His ears were trained on another sound, a soft rustling of leaves, a third set of footfalls. He had heard it only momentarily, but to Barney's well-honed senses, once was enough verification. He stalked.

"Barney, no!" Denise called to him, trying to keep her voice at a whisper. "It is almost dawn. Someone will see us returning. De Culo's men will report us. Come," she pleaded. "Please."

There was no one in the immediate vicinity, although Barney knew that the dense, water-laden earth and the starless night could twist and change sounds like a ventriloquist so that you couldn't pinpoint a noise with any exactitude, no matter how carefully you listened. For all he knew, the vague rustling of heavy leaves he heard could have originated a mile or more away.

As he stood helplessly, listening for another noise, Denise came over to him, her eyes sad and frightened, her legs and patterned skirt smeared with black mud. She put her hand on his arm. "Let us go, my husband," she said. "Before it is too late."

Reluctantly, Barney replaced his pistol in its holster and followed her out.

Then, deep in the jungle, a voice sighed, a tangle of rubber plants rustled freely, a small white hand wiped a band of beaded perspiration from beneath a white-blonde brow, and then Gloria was running in a straight, familiar course toward the gleaming mouth of the mountain installation.

Safe again in her kitchen with the dawn pouring through the wavy glass of the windows like a rainbow, Denise wrapped her arms around her husband and kissed him on his mouth.

"I am glad you came back with me," she said, smiling. "I was afraid for a moment that our son would be without a father before he was even born."

Barney felt his heartbeat skip. "Our son?" he asked quietly.

She took his hand and led it lovingly to her belly. It was still taut, but when Barney looked into her eyes, he could see that they were glowing and full of promise and new life.

"Denise," he said, laughing as he picked her up in his arms like a doll and twirled her around the room. "Oh, Denise. I didn't think I could ever love you more than I did yesterday morning. Now I love you twice as much."

"He is still so tiny," she said, kissing his neck as a tear slid down her cheek and into her mouth. Then she laughed. "Oh, look at us, kissing like two street beggars. We are as dirty as the banana pickers during the big rains."

"You're the cleanest, most perfect thing that's ever come into my life," Barney said. And he led her to the bedroom they had shared for love many times before. He set her on the edge of the bed and knelt to kiss her face and unbuttoned her ruffled blouse. It fell off one shoulder. He brought his lips to her creamy, golden skin and brushed them against her.

This woman, he thought, so good, so warm and ready, all the woman he would ever want. This woman was his.

He loved her then, on the big squeaky bed, this clean woman who carried his baby and would love him for all time. He loved her between her strong legs and counted himself among the richest men.

121

When they were finished and she lay flushed and satisfied in his arms, he kissed her closed eyes and said, "Aren't you going to ask me what I did with the girl yesterday? The blonde?"

"No. I am not going to ask."

"Afraid, huh?" he teased.

"Not afraid. I knew you had business to do. You would not stop loving me for a whore."

He pressed her hand in his. "I couldn't stop loving you for anyone or anything," he said. "I couldn't if I tried. But I want you to know I didn't do anything with her."

"Why not?" she asked, new worry lines creasing her face. "Now she will be suspicious."

Barney shrugged. "I found out what I needed to know. Besides, she was too repulsive. Something pale and snaky about her." He shuddered. "I don't know. I just couldn't do it. It would have been like rubbing up against a disease."

"That was very stupid of you. You will have to leave Hispania immediately."

"Not without you, I won't."

"I've got to sell the business."

"To hell with the business."

"It's worth $20,000 American."

"To hell with $20,000 American."

"Oh, you are so stupid, Barney."

"Yeah? Well, I happen to think I'm the smartest guy in the world." He tickled her. After all, I ended up with you, didn't I? I think that qualifies me for some heavy honors."

"Barney," she giggled. "Stop that."

"I must be the smartest, luckiest, happiest guy who ever lived, and you are coming with me to Washington tomorrow, where I will turn in my picture and get a nice, boring job that will keep me alive long enough to see our son grown and making his own mistakes. How does that sound?"

She hugged him hard. "Barney," she said, her eyes flashing sparks of gold.

"What?"

"I will go."

"You better. You're my wife."

"I will make coffee."

"What for? Get us packed. I'll go into town and make the arrangements."

"First we will have coffee," she said.

There were no beans for coffee in the kitchen.

"Forget the coffee," Barney said.

"No. I will buy the beans."

"Send someone for them."

"No. I know the right beans."

"You're the most stubborn woman I've ever met," he said as she wrapped a light shawl around her shoulders.

"Are you sorry you married me, my husband?"

Barney smiled. "No. I'm not sorry."

"Then I will get the beans."

Barney shook his head as she walked out the door. He set two cups on the table in preparation. He brought out two spoons. He poured milk into a colorful ceramic pitcher, which Denise said her mother had given her. He spooned the brown, coarse sugar into a thick bowl.

He waited.

An hour later, he walked into the garden to pick an orchid for the table. He placed it in a miniature vase Denise had bought a few days before.

He lit a cigarette. He waited.

Within another hour, Barney knew he would never see his wife again.

Instead, someone hurled a piece of her cotton

shawl, torn and bloodied, through the window. Smeared on the shawl was a small brownish-red pulp. There was a note attached: "This is your wife and child."

The reddish pulp turned out to be tissue from Denise's uterus. Whoever had killed her had ripped open her belly to kill her baby. Barney's baby.

With a scream of vengeance, he worked his way through the house, destroying everything in his path. He saved the blonde girl's room for last. She was not there. As punishment for her not being there, Barney smashed every item in the room until every shred of furniture, of clothing, of glass was indistinguishable from every other.

Then he began.

He walked the streets quietly, looking, searching, hoping no stranger would approach him to talk, because he would kill anyone who came within killing distance of him. No one approached.

He entered the rain forest.

This time, when the sound came, he was ready. It was a clumsy sound, deliberate. If Barney were thinking, he would have known it was a trap. The sound had been too careless for a mistake. But the rage inside Barney heard the sound before his intellect did, and his rage responded eagerly, wantonly. He wanted to kill. He wanted to die.

The first man to show himself, a dark, squat young man who teetered out of the bush hesitantly, got a bullet square in the abdomen. The second caught one in the middle of his face.

Barney's rage fed on it. The sight of the man's features exploding into a fountain of blood drove him forward, wanting more.

Out of the corner of his eye he spotted a curved killing knife, the kind the jungle natives carved from gypsum found deep in a mountain's interior, flying above him in an arc. He ducked and rolled at just the moment when it would have sliced off the top of his head, and fired randomly into the bush. A wayward arm popped into view, then dropped heavily to the ground with a dying scream. It rang out in the wet forest, a fading echo that came from every direction and mingled with the frightened bird sounds before surrendering to the vacuum silence.

He walked over to the nearest dead man, who lay on his back, an expression of benign surprise on his face. His stomach was covered with blood, already congealing in the ferocious swampy heat. Barney kicked him.

Silence. They were all dead. Only three men. Then he knew it was a trap.

He could feel the eyes now, dozens of them, waiting in silence for Barney to empty the rest of his bullets into dispensable recruits. It was a trap, but he didn't care.

He fired three times into the air, then tossed the revolver to the side. "Come get me, you bastards!" he called.

"Bastards . . . Bastards . . . Bastards," the jungle echoed all around him.

"This is Bernard C. Daniels of the United States of America, and I am going to kill your president, so you had better come and take me to him," he called in Spanish.

"Gladly," a voice answered in English. A fat man gaudily dressed in a fairytale uniform of blue and gold and a feathered tricorn hat straightened his knees with great difficulty and rose from behind a eucalyptus tree. "You will come with me, Mr. Daniels of the Central Intelligence Agency," he said.

The officer snapped an order to the bushes and

trees around him, and twenty-odd men, their bodies barely covered by ragged shards of cloth, appeared from nowhere. They were all young men, Barney noticed. Hungry men. They avoided his stare. Many of them had known Denise, he guessed. But hunger is a greater motivation than friendship.

He spat in the face of a young man who tied his wrists together with thick rope. The man said nothing.

"I curse your wife and child," Barney said softly in Spanish. He could feel the man's hands trembling as he completed the knot. "They will die as my wife has died."

The man backed away, fear gripping his features.

"Get him moving," the officer ordered. Someone shoved Barney ahead. The man who had tied the rope around his wrists stood rooted to his spot, shaking.

"You. Move," the officer called. The man did not move.

The officer drew a gigantic magnum from a holster strapped to his thigh and fired point-blank at the young soldier. His chest opened up like a red, smoking mouth as he was thrust backward by the force of the bullet, his legs stretching out in front of him. The blast propelled his dying body into the ranks of the other soldiers. One screamed. "The cursed one," he screamed. "I have been touched by the blood of the cursed one!"

Quickly the other soldiers ran ahead, leaving him isolated and panicked, trying desperately to wipe the dead man's blood from his hands and chest.

The officer fired another shot and dropped him in his tracks. "Stupid jungle beasts," the officer said. "Move the prisoner along."

Mumbling to one another, soldiers guided Barney

126

to the mountain cave. At the entrance they dropped behind as the officer grabbed the rope around Barney's wrists and raised his magnum to Barney's temple. "Blindfold him," he commanded, and a man rushed forward with a scrap of roughly woven cloth to tie around his eyes.

Barney stumbled in darkness around the cave, noting its enormous size from the distance of sounds inside. There was almost no human noise within the installation, he noticed. Either none of the soldiers recruited from Puerta del Rey was permitted inside, or the discipline of De Culo's army was tremendous. The noise all originated from machinery, vast amounts of it, some small and whirring, some huge and powerful, belching with the drone of earth movers. The place was still growing, still making room for more equipment and ammunition . . . or for something even bigger.

He was shoved into a room to the left of all the noise, where the air was drier and more welcoming. A door sealed precisely behind him. He was pushed downward into a hard wooden chair. The blindfold was removed.

In front of him sat a small man behind a desk. His thin hair was combed forward in neoclassical curls. His uniform, like that of the officer who brought Barney to this place, was blue and white, and of antique military design. Yards of gold braid adorned his epaulets. A jeweler's case of ancient military decorations gleamed across his chest. A silken banner of red, white, and blue slashed a diagonal line from shoulder to waist. On a table beside the desk rested an exact replica of Napoleon's battle headdress, trimmed with ostrich plumes.

As the slight, round-faced man rose from behind his massive desk, he slid his right hand into the closure of his coat, just beneath the second button. He smiled, his hard, intelligent eyes sparkling.

"I am El Presidente Cara De Culo," he said, his neck craning to posture in an aristocratic profile. "And this is General Robar Estomago, chief of the Hispanian police. The general informs us that you seek audience."

"I'm going to kill you, pig," Barney said.

"Said like a true American, Mr. Daniels. In truth, it is I who seek audience with you. I sincerely hope you will be able to spare a small amount of time to speak with me and my men about your—shall we say—activities in our island paradise." He opened a drawer of his desk and produced Barney's camera. He opened the back of it and extracted the film.

"I am given to understand that this contains photographs of this installation," he said, holding the roll daintily between forefinger and thumb. "I am flattered that a representative of such a technologically advanced nation as yours would exhibit an interest in our small makeshift enterprise. However, I regret to inform you that we are not yet prepared for publicity pictures. They would not convey the correct impression of the base. Dirt in the corners, incomplete molding, that sort of thing. You understand. Bad public relations. No, unfortunately, these cannot be shown to your friends in Washington."

His smile froze on his face, he yanked the film from its cylinder. "Alas," he said softly, "the pictures are spoiled." He swept the camera to the floor with a flick of his hand.

Slowly, De Culo circled his desk to stand in front of Barney. He folded his arms in front of him. He rested his chin on his fist. He stared into Barney's eyes. "So you see," he said in his quiet, brooding voice, "now that the film you took has been de-

128

stroyed, the only evidence the world will have that our installation exists will be based on your testimony. I presume you intend to inform your superiors about the events of the past several days, Mr. Daniels?"

"Go fuck yourself."

"I amend my question. I do not presume you will return to America with this information. In point of fact, Mr. Daniels, I do not believe you will return to America at all. If I may hazard a guess, I predict that you will be quite dead in rather a short time." He smiled again, a chilling, humorless smile. "Or a longer time. That will be up to you. Of course, my men will welcome the opportunity to converse with you first. We wish to know to what extent your government is aware of Hispania's relations to other world powers." He held up a hand quickly. "Now, Mr. Daniels, I'm sure you do not wish to be pressed on this matter, so I would not think of asking you to reveal this information to me immediately. You will have ample opportunity, as our guest, to talk with us whenever you wish."

In the corner, General Robar Estomago snickered. "Silence, jackass," De Culo hissed. The general snapped to attention.

"Before you retire to our guest room, however, I would like to tell you that we have been aware of your actions for some time. Through the initiative of General Estomago here, we learned that you had probably seen a map detailing some information which was not for public perusal. We also knew about your photographic expedition here, about your desire to leave the country. My, my. The very walls have ears. We even knew about your pitiful little wedding to the village whore."

Barney leapt to his feet. "You pig-sucking mur-

129

derer!" he screamed. Estomago knocked him into the chair again and pulled Barney's blindfold tight around his throat. "I'll—kill—you," he gurgled in spite of the pressure around his neck.

De Culo laughed.

The pressure eased. "What have you done with my wife?" Barney demanded.

De Culo shrugged. "Why, haven't you heard, Mr. Daniels? She met with a dreadful accident."

"The body," Barney managed. "Where is the body?"

"Nowhere special. A ditch, perhaps, or a swamp. Where she belongs."

This time, Barney moved before Estomago could restrain him. With one leap, he hurled himself toward De Culo and placed an expert kick at his head. But the president ducked in time and took the blow in the meaty part of his back. Still, it staggered him and he reeled crazily into the corner of the room. Barney didn't have another chance. Estomago's magnum was drawn and lodged inside his mouth before he could rise from the spot on the floor where he had fallen.

"Take the American scum away," De Culo said, doubled over from the pain in his back. Estomago yanked Barney to his feet.

"Wait," De Culo shouted as the two men reached the door. "There is one more thing I wish to give our guest. A welcoming gift." His eyes vicious, he stumbled over to the desk and threw open a drawer. "I was saving this for later, but I think that now would be perfectly appropriate."

He reached deep into the drawer and pulled out something soft and ashen. He tossed it toward Barney. It hit him on the cheek, feeling like a cold leather bag, then dropped to the floor.

And there, at his feet, rested Denise's severed hand, its thin gold wedding band still encircling the third finger.

"She wouldn't take the ring off," De Culo spat. "So we took it off for her. Get him out of my sight."

Dazed, Barney allowed himself to be dragged out of the room where De Culo's laughter grew louder and louder, where the little hand with its cheap ring lay on the floor.

She wouldn't take it off, Barney said to himself as he felt himself being shoved into a small stone cell dripping with cave water. Two rats scurried into the corners at the intrusion. A solid door closed slowly and finally, first narrowing the light to a thin line and then obliterating it.

He sat on the cold stone floor in the darkness, with the squealing of the rats behind him, and thought only: She wouldn't take my ring off.

# CHAPTER TWELVE

SWEENEY, GLORIA P.

B. 1955, BILOXI, MISS.
ATTENDANCE, FARMINGTON CO. ELE-
    MENTARY
OCC: NONE

INCARCERATION: MISS. STATE PENI-
TENTIARY, 1973–76

SUB (1) INCARCERATION

MANSLAUGHTER, DEGREE 1, 15 YRS.-
    LIFE, COMMUTED WHEN SUBJECT
    SUBMITTED TO VOLUNTARY WORK
    PROGRAM IN PUERTA DEL REY, HIS-
    PANIA, 1978

Harold W. Smith stopped the printout. "I think
I've found her," he said into the phone. "Hold on,
Remo."

He keyed in:

SUB (2) VOLUNTARY WORK PROGRAM,
    PUERTA DEL REY.

INSTITUTED 1978 BY      ESTOMAGO,
    GEN. ROBAR S.,

CHIEF, NATL SECURITY COUNCIL,
    CURR. AMBASSADOR
TO U.S. VOL. WORK PROGRAM FOR
    FEMALE PRISON INMATES IN LIEU
    OF MAXIMUM SENTENCE. NATURE
    OF WORK: DOMESTIC.
NUMBER:
(1978) 47
(1979) 38
(1980) 39

"That's odd," Smith said, stopping the machine.
"What's odd?" Remo asked. "Look, I don't have

all day to hang on the phone while you play tunes on your computer. There's still the business of Denise Daniels and some kind of map on Gloria Sweeney's wall and some mosque somewhere—"

"The mosque is at 128-26 West 114th Street," Smith said. "If Denise Daniels was Barney's wife, that's nothing to worry about," he muttered offhandedly. "Just a personal matter. Naturally, he would have been concerned by her death, so he would have opened the envelope with the bomb in it, since it carried her name on the return address. It was obviously intended for Daniels, although Max Snodgrass beat him to it. But in itself, this Denise Daniels is really . . . nothing . . ."

He trailed off as his eye caught the last line of the printout. "Remo, when Daniels was talking, did he say anything about seeing a lot of American women on the island?"

"Only Gloria Sweeney."

"Funny. The CIA doesn't have any records about them, either. According to this printout, there are at least 120 female American prison inmates in Puerta del Rey."

"I didn't know there were prisons in Puerta del Rey. I thought they shot criminals first and tried them later."

"That's not far from the truth," Smith said. "Nevertheless, Gloria Sweeney was sent to Hispania as a prisoner serving a life sentence. She's back in the States now, illegally. My guess is that she's involved with Estomago, the Hispanian ambassador."

"Then why all the black freedom business, and the Peaches of Mecca and all that? And why did she have Calder Raisin killed? And what about the map Daniels keeps hollering about?"

133

"I have a theory or two, but nothing substantial. You find that out," Smith said. "I have to scan some prison records. Remo?"

"What?"

"Be quick about it." He hung up.

It could be nothing. All of the information gathered so far through Smith's records and Barney's delirious testimony, might mean nothing more than that the leadership of a dissatisfied banana republic decided to make America uncomfortable by stirring up its black population. Just another case of the mouse chewing between the elephant's toes.

But some of the printouts Smith had pulled from the CURE computer banks late the night before didn't sit well. Like the three bulletins from American air surveillance over the Atlantic confirming the presence of Russian freighters heading toward Cuba. Or the flutter of activity on banana boats between Hispania and Cuba. There had been too many incidences of Hispanian boats getting lost in Cuban waters for Smith to accept, especially since neither Hispania nor Cuba needed to trade bananas with one another.

There was nothing definite, nothing to cause anything more than idle speculation on the part of Dr. Harold W. Smith.

Idle speculation, Smith repeated to himself as he keyed in the code for penitentiary inmate files. Still, time should not be wasted. He made a point of accelerating his typing speed from forty words a minute to forty-three.

# CHAPTER THIRTEEN

Barney was starving.

Had it been a week? A month? No, he reasoned, with what was left of his reason. He couldn't go a month without food.

One thing he knew for certain: his water was drugged. After his first screaming, shaking experience with the water, he tried to ignore the little metal pan that slid through a rubber opening onto a small shelf in his cave cell, but when his thirst overcame him he drank. He took as little as possible to moisten his parched, raw mouth and throat because he knew that after he drank, he would have to submit to the dreams.

Terrible dreams they were, confusing, nonsensical hallucinations that stabbed at his brain and burned it from inside. When they came, he tried to remember Denise, Denise in her kitchen, Denise making coffee. Denise kept him alive through the dreams while he convulsed and retched and screamed. She watched him. She smiled. She comforted.

It must be a month, Barney thought as he dabbed one finger onto the surface of the water and carried the drop to his lips. The drug was less virulent at the top of the pan, Barney learned, if he let it sit. He allowed himself no more than ten drops every time he drank, and he drank as infrequently as possible. Still, the dreams and nausea passed through him like air through a screen, and there was nothing Barney could do except to summon the name of his dead wife.

"Denise," he whispered. "Help me."

Light appeared. For the first time in the countless days of absolute darkness since he was first brought to his cell, the door opened.

The flash of high-wattage interior lighting hurt his eyes. He shielded them. "Come," a voice said. So loud. It sounded like cannons to Barney's sound-deprived ears.

Hands groped for him on the cold slime of the floor. He tried to pull himself to his feet. He couldn't stand.

Outside, he curled himself into a tight ball to protect his eyes from the blinding light. A boot kicked him in the groin. "Move."

With the help of four men, Barney stumbled through a vast empty-sounding cave, his eyes closed for fear of being blinded, and out into the welcome darkness of the jungle.

Barney heard the jungle, teeming with noise. The flapping of birds' wings. Their songs. The piercing wails of animals dying miles away. The rustle of salamanders on leaves fallen to the earth. The earth itself exploded with sound: the rush of wind from the ocean, the music of moving water. And the smell. The wonderful smell of green things. The smell of life.

"Water," he said. "*Agua. Agua.*"

The young men escorting him turned to their commander, a swarthy guerrilla in Cuban-style fa-

136

tigues and combat boots. He was the only one besides Barney who wore shoes.

"Move," the soldier repeated, pushing Barney forward.

For a moment, Barney's eyes met those of a young barefoot recruit to his right. He was still a boy, no more than sixteen. The boy's eyes were sad. They reminded him of Denise.

*"Es nada,"* Barney said to him. "It is nothing."

The jungle grew more dense, until only an incidental patch of sky could be seen at the very tops of the trees. Ahead, Barney spotted a small fire.

It glowed like a coal in the darkness, becoming brighter as the squadron dragged him toward it. The fire was in a thatched bamboo hut. Inside the hut, a cot waited for Barney.

His shoes were removed and he was tied down with hemp rope. The young recruit with the sad eyes stoked the fire. Why they felt Barney needed a fire in the sweltering heat of the jungle was beyond him. Then they left him alone.

At nightfall, the music of the jungle changed. The chattering beguine of the day birds gave way to the more somber, dangerous rhythms of night. Night was for the screams of vultures, the ravenous compaints of the big cats.

It was at night that El Presidente Cara De Culo came to Barney.

"Fancy meeting you here, Mr. Daniels," he said smoothly. "Isn't it a small world?" He waited for an answer. Barney could no longer speak.

"I see you're not feeling talkative this evening. Too bad. I was hoping your days of relaxation might prompt you to participate in a discussion of your country. Rather for old times' sake, you know.

After all, someday soon it may not exist any more. Tsk, tsk. Things come and they go, don't they Mr. Daniels?"

He sighed. "Yes, they come and they go. Just like your dear, departed wife. Remember her? The one who spread her legs for half the island?"

Barney closed his eyes. Denise in the kitchen making coffee, Denise smiling.

"She went so badly, too," De Culo said with mock concern. "First the hand. Ugh, ghastly. Nothing uglier than a screaming woman with a bloody stump for an arm."

Denise in her shawl, Denise carrying his baby.

"Then, of course, she was still alive when the men raped her. Boys will be boys, you know. Although I think she secretly enjoyed it. They all do, the experts say."

"Denise," Barney croaked, the dry sobs racking him.

"As a matter of fact, I distinctly remember someone telling me she was alive when the knife cut her open. Apparently she called out 'my baby' or some such drivel. God only knows who the father was."

"I will kill you if it takes all my life and the next," Barney said slowly, the words rasping out of him like rusted nails.

"Very poetic," De Culo said, smiling. "Well, I must be off. I only stopped by to bring you another present. You left the first on my office floor. Perhaps this will be more to your liking."

He picked an iron poker up off the floor and thrust it into the fire. "These are rare around here," he said. "It's from my own personal fireplace. I want you to know that."

Then he stood over Barney and with both hands bashed the lower part of his abdomen. "Stinking

138

slime," De Culo said. "I'll see to it you stay alive as long as possible."

"I'll stay alive long enough to kill you," Barney wheezed, his belly knotted and cramping violently from the blow.

Within a half hour, Estomago entered, along with the four men who had brought him to the hut. Once again, the young boy with the sad eyes was with them. Once again he stoked the already blazing fire.

Estomago loosened the top button of his uniform and ran a finger along his red, sweating neck. "It's hot as hell in here," he said to no one in particular. He looked down at Barney, shriveled to almost half his weight, his wrists raw and bleeding from the rope around them.

"Water," Barney rasped.

"No water," Estomago said. "It is not permitted."

The boy stoking the fire looked over to the two of them.

"This is a bad way to die," Estomago said without a trace of De Culo's sarcasm. "Tell us who else knows about the installation, and I will see that you die quickly, with a bullet."

It would have been so easy for Barney to tell him the truth, that the United States knew nothing about the installation. He would die then. It would all be over.

But he could not die. Not until De Culo was dead. Not until his wife's death had been avenged.

"Let me go," Barney said. "Then I will tell you."

Estomago shook his head. "I cannot do that. You must die, soon or late."

"Late," Barney said.

"As you wish." He motioned to the soldier in army fatigues. "Dominquez. The whip."

The soldier approached Barney's cot, a long lizard whip in his hands. He tapped it on his palm expertly, a small smile of anticipation playing on his face.

Estomago moved out of the way.

Slowly, with sensuous pleasure, the soldier teased Barney's skin with the end of the whip. It glistened irridescent green in the light of the fire as it snaked across Barney's chest and legs. The soldier began to breathe heavily. His lips moved, wet with saliva. His eyes half-closed as he played the whip on Barney's genitals. Then he raised the whip, and, with a cry of pleasure, let it fly with a skin-splitting crack on Barney's belly.

*Denise. Oh, help me, Denise.*

The soldier raised the whip again, his own sex now obviously hard and throbbing, and threw out his arm to his right. The whip coiled and sank into the tender skin on the insteps of Barney's feet.

Sparks flew inside Barney's brain. The pain was aflame, burning, burning. Endless pain. *Denise. Don't go. Don't leave me.*

The whip snapped high overhead. It slashed him between his legs.

Up from the pit of his stomach, black bile gushed from Barney's mouth and bubbled on his lips. Then he was unconscious.

In a fury, the soldier tore his canteen from his belt and threw its contents on Barney's face to bring him back to consciousness. "You will not sleep now," he roared in almost incoherent Spanish. "Not until I am finished."

Barney's tongue reached for the droplets of water on his face, the pain returning with horrible intensity. The soldier beat him again and again, each time bringing the whip down with the force of a lover's thrust. "Now!" he screamed. "Now!" He curled the

140

whip in a giant loop that circled the ceiling and brought it down so that it caught the length of Barney's torn body and sent it into convulsive spasms.

As Barney's muscles jerked in reflexive agony, the soldier bucked and groaned until he lay spent on the dirt floor, moaning with pleasure.

Barney did not regain consciousness for several hours. He came to with the taste of cold mountain water trickling down his throat. He sputtered and coughed, but kept drinking, for fear that it would be taken away before he could drink enough to stay alive through the night. Hands that smelled of earth and green plants smoothed more of the water on Barney's eyes and forehead.

He opened his eyes. The boy whose job it had been to stoke the fire in the hut made a signal for him to be silent, and gave him another bowl of water to drink.

"I will not forget you, my son," Barney muttered in Spanish. Immediately a rustling sound outside the hut alerted him to the fact that guards were posted. The boy ducked. The guard peered inside. "He's delirious," he said to an invisible comrade, and went back to his watch.

The boy made a face at Barney as he got up off the floor, then offered him the bowl once again. Barney shook his head. The boy doused his wounds with the water left in the bowl, warning Barney not to cry out in pain.

It hurt, but Barney would not let the boy be killed for helping him. He held his breath and let the water do its work. Then the boy slithered through a slim crack in the rushes of the hut and was gone.

The days went on. The beatings, the interrogations, the whip. Always the whip. Each day, a man would appear with a clamp to break one of Barney's fingers. And each night, the whip.

"What does the CIA know?"

"Eat shit."

"What have you told them?"

"That your mother is a whore."

"Are there any other agents hidden on the island?"

"May your rectum be a pool for the love juice of ditchdiggers."

Sometimes Barney spoke in English, sometimes in Spanish. It didn't matter. As long as he spoke. As long as he stayed alive.

After all of his fingers were broken, Estomago gave him water. It was the drugged water of the cave prison, poisoned and fearful. It made the dreams come.

He began to have a special dream, one that recurred with predictable regularity. The dream was of women.

Each night since he was forced to drink the drugged water, a host of beautiful women, naked and shimmering in the firelight, danced into the hut and surrounded him, smoothing their fragrant hands on his face, rubbing their breasts and lips on him. Each night they came and left without a word, to return the next night, feathery and lovely.

The beatings stopped. He was given water four times a day. During the daylight hours, the soldiers would come to stoke the fire and give him water, and at night they were replaced by the women, smiling, dancing, tantalizing.

He began to heal. His rope-burned wrists were bandaged, so that his only bondage was a rope around one ankle. He began to crave the water.

The dreams were not so terrible any more. They

were pleasant. Confusing, crazy, colorful dreams. Who cared? What was so great about reality, anyway? Barney looked forward to his four bowls of water. They made the world fuzzy and pretty. They made the world nice.

Even the soldiers were nice. They began to smile at him. They brought him food, first an easily digestible paste made of mashed vegetables, then soft bread and fruit, then good meals of army rations. And throughout all the dishes was laced the delicious dreams in the water.

Everyone smiled. Everyone was happy. Except for the young boy who stoked the fire. What was with him, anyway, always staring at Barney as if he worried the sky was going to fall? Such a worry wart, for such a young boy. Maybe he was just a gringo hater. Well, it took all kinds of people to make a world, good and bad, and what difference did it make, anyway?

Barney began to wonder what life was like outside the hut. Had he ever been outside? It seemed that his world began and ended there, in that thatched roof paradise with the wonderful water. Well, that was fine with him. Especially if the women kept coming around.

They did. Now they spoke to him, too, sweet words of comfort and flirtation.

"We like you very much," a very blonde girl said. Did she look familiar? Of course, she had been coming into the hut since day one. *No,* a voice inside Barney said. *Familiar from somewhere else. Get lost,* Barney told his voice. *There is nowhere else.* The voice went away.

"I like you too," Barney said happily. "I like everything."

"Well, I'm going to do something you'll like

extra-special," the thin blonde said, and the other girls giggled.

"Oh, boy," Barney said, clapping his hands together. "What is it? A cookie?"

"Better than that, honey." She knelt between his legs and took him in her mouth, rocking, pulling, sending shivers up his back with her naughty little tongue.

"Gee whiz," Barney said. "You sure were right. This beats just about anything. Think I could have some water?"

"Sure, angel," another woman said, and gave him a big, long drink. It made everything even better.

Then, before he knew it, a whole lot of other gorgeous naked women were making love to him, too, laughing, probing, kissing, touching. And all he had to do was lie there and drink that magic water. Heaven on earth.

They played games. If Barney won the game, the women would see to it that he felt good. If he lost the game, they would make him feel good anyway. The games were fun.

"Okay," the blonde girl said one night. "I have a new game to play."

"Oh, boy," Barney said.

"First, you may have water."

"Yea." Barney drank. "I drank it all down," he said proudly.

"That's a very good boy, Barney."

"Good good Barney," the girls chanted in chorus of approval. Barney beamed. He knew this was going to be a fun game.

"Now, I'm going to say a word, and then you say the first thing that comes. Okay?"

"Sure," Barney said. "That's easy."

"Good. Now here's the word. Ready?"

Barney nodded enthusiastically.

"Girls."

"Fun," Barney said, rolling his eyes. The women all laughed.

"That's correct, Barney," the blonde said. "Girls are fun. Now, here's another word."

"Ready, set, go."

"Okay. El Presidente Cara De Culo."

"Huh?"

"De Culo."

"I don't know that word," Barney said, his face squishing up to burst into tears.

"There, there," the blonde girl said, stroking Barney's head. "It's all right. That was a hard word." The rest of the women made sympathetic noises. "I'll tell you what it means, and then you can say the right thing, okay?"

"I love you," Barney said.

"You little sweet thing. El Presidente Cara De Culo is the greatest man on earth. Who is he?"

"The greatest," Barney said.

"Wonderful. You get a kiss." All the women milled around to kiss him. "Ready for another word?"

"Sure."

The blonde looked into his eyes. "Denise," she said. The women were silent as Barney struggled with his thoughts.

At last, his face lit up. "I got it! I got it!"

"What?" the blonde woman asked flatly, her eyes cold.

"De niece is de daughter of de uncle," Barney said. And everyone kissed and hugged him.

"That's wonderful, Barney. You're such a smart boy."

"You bet."

"How about this? CIA."

"CIA?" Barney was confused. "I think I work for the CIA." He stuck his finger in his nose to think. "But I don't work. I play."

"You used to work for them, darling. But they were bad, bad people."

"Very bad?"

"Awful. They beat you up."

"The soldiers beat me up."

"They did not!" The women frowned. Some turned their backs on him. "You're bad, Barney. Bad for thinking the soldiers hurt you."

"They whipped me with the big snake. They hurt my hands," Barney said helplessly.

"That was the CIA. Not the soldiers."

Barney's eyes widened in confusion. He was sure it was the soldiers. "Maybe they were different soldiers," he offered.

"That's right," the blonde said, brightening. All the women kissed him. "Good Barney," they said.

"Yeah. Other soldiers. CIA soldiers. Bad."

"De Culo, the greatest man on earth, made them stop. Now soldiers are nice to you."

"De Culo good, CIA bad," Barney said.

"The CIA is still near," the woman whispered.

"Here? Here?"

"Yes."

"Where?" He looked anxiously around the room.

"We don't know. Tell us, Barney. Tell us where they are, so they don't come again to hurt you."

"I—I don't know. What's the answer, lady?"

"Come on. You know."

"Huh-unh." Barney shook his head vehemently.

"Maybe he's the only one," the woman said quietly to her associates. "Okay," she said louder. "Here's another word."

146

"I'm tired of this game."

"Just one more. Installation."

Barney yawned. "Installation is what daddy puts around the house to keep out the snow," he said. "Hey, when's it going to snow?"

The women ignored him, chattering among themselves.

"That's all, Barney. You've been a good boy."

"How about some ficky-fick?"

"Later, sweetheart. We have to look for CIA men, so they don't come to harm our Barney."

"CIA bad," Barney confirmed. "Ficky-fick good."

"Drink some water," the blonde said, and led the women outside.

"He doesn't know anything," the blonde later told Estomago. "You might as well kill him and get it over with."

"El Presidente wants us to go through with this."

"It's pointless."

"But it is a direct order, Gloria."

Gloria Sweeney shrugged. "Have it your way."

"My way keeps you out of working at the installation, remember," Estomago said with a threatening swagger.

"Yeah. Thanks a heap, big shot. I suppose working at that whorehouse was your idea of a great career opportunity."

"Better than being shot, like the other women. Or perhaps you would prefer their fate."

A nervous tingle shot through Gloria's spine. "Not at all, Robar, honey. You know I was just joshing. I'm grateful for everything you've done for me." She caressed his thigh. "And I just love being sweet to you."

"That's enough," Estomago said, clearing his throat. "We'll save it for later."

"Anytime you say, jumbo." She left him to bathe in a stream and wash the stink of fear off her.

That night, a soldier wearing a big painted sign reading *CIA* hanging around his neck entered the hut to remove Barney's fingernails.

The next night, another soldier, similarly identified, came to beat him within an inch of his life.

The food stopped coming. The women stopped coming. The smiles ceased. Only the water remained. And the smoldering fire.

Bound again by abrasive rope around his wrists, Barney cried and asked for his mother.

"We hate your mother," a soldier said, and slapped him hard across the face. "This is what the CIA thinks of you and your mother. Your mother fucks gorillas."

"CIA bad, bad," Barney wailed.

"You didn't tell the good soldiers that we were here," the soldier said, "so we came to hurt you."

Barney looked from face to face around the hut. They were all in there with him, all the soldiers and women. They shook their heads sadly as the bad CIA man walked deliberately to the fire and removed the glowing poker.

"The CIA is going to hurt you now unless you tell us where the other CIA men are."

"Don't know," Barney said as the man walked closer and closer to him, the poker gleaming red.

"We're very bad men," he said, stepping so close that Barney could smell the burning cypress wood sticking to the end of the poker. "We want you to remember who we are."

"CIA," Barney said. "Very bad."

The soldier lifted the poker directly above Barney's stomach. "Very bad," he said. "For you." And he brought it down to trace the letters *CIA* on Barney's burning belly, the stench of incinerated flesh filling the hut as Barney screamed his last memories away.

Two days later, Barney's eyes opened to see the barrel of a magnum pointed directly at them.

"He knows nothing," Estomago said. "Let us end this charade now and be done with it."

"Hey, I've got an idea," Gloria said. "Want to have some fun with him before he goes?"

"Fun. You always think of fun."

"No, really. This'll be a gas." She whispered into Estomago's ear.

He laughed. "Why not?" he said, tucking the magnum back into his thigh holster. "It will be amusing for the men."

He shook Barney out of the fog that had come back to reclaim him. "You. Get up. You are free."

"Free?" Barney said, not sure what the word meant.

The soldiers unbound his wrists and led him, wobbling, to the grounds outside the hut. There they tied another length of rope around one arm, this time a longer, thinner one.

"You will perform the ritual of the bat," Estomago said. "For it, you will fight a man while blindfolded and bound to him by this length of rope. If you kill him, you will be set free."

"Fight," Barney mumbled, looking vaguely at the red gashes on his stomach which had already filled up with pus.

The blonde woman giggled. "Find him someone cute to fight, honey. That'll make it more interesting."

Estomago pointed to the young recruit with the sad eyes. "Him?"

"Perfect."

He signalled the boy to advance. Silently he came into the circle where Barney waited, weaving unsteadily on his feet. The boy's arm was tied to the rope. Blindfolds were placed on both men.

"Here are the knives," Estomago announced, placing a curved killing knife in each of their hands. "When I give the command, the two of you will fight to the death." He turned to one of the soldiers. "Get your rifle ready," he said quietly. "If the American should win by a freak accident, I do not want him to leave alive."

"Yes sir." The soldier obeyed, disengaging the safety catch on his rifle.

"Very well," Estomago shouted. "Begin!"

In a crouch, the boy circled Barney, who poked hesitantly at the air. The crowd laughed.

"Hsss!" the boy whispered. "This way." He led Barney to the edge of the circle. The spectators cleared the way. He slashed at Barney, narrowly missing him, even though Barney could barely walk.

"That boy fights almost as poorly as the American," Estomago said, his belly shaking with mirth.

The boy slashed again, this time falling to the ground and rolling close to the jungle edge.

"Birds," Barney said.

"We are close to the forest," the boy whispered. "Pretend to fight me. I will take you out of here." He cut into the air again and inched closer to the edge of the clearing.

Barney fell.

"Kill him, kill him!" the women in the crowd shouted.

150

The boy lunged. "Get up. Quickly. Hurry. It is time."

Barney scrambled to his feet as the crowd crooned with excitement. "Perhaps he will give us a show, after all," Estomago said. "But you are both too far away for us to see well," he shouted to the two men. "Come back this way."

"Now," the boy said, tearing off his blindfold and Barney's. "Try to keep up with me." He sprinted through the jungle like a gazelle on his long young legs while Barney dragged behind, the rope forcing him to keep pace. "Come." Two shots rang out behind them.

Branches tore at Barney's open wounds. Each step burned his damaged feet like hot coals. His broken hands could barely hold the knife, but he knew he must hold it. He knew nothing any more, remembered nothing except that this boy was a friend and that he had to hold on to the knife and run, run as he had never run before.

The boy cut the rope between them. "I know a small clearing not far from here," he said. "You can rest there, and drink good water to make you well." He pushed Barney ahead.

At the clearing, where a small waterfall fed into a stream from underground caves, they stopped. "Do not drink yet," the boy said. "We will wait in the cave for nightfall. Estomago's men are not far behind."

Barney opened and shut his eyes to try to clear his head. Everything was filmy, unreal. "Trust me," the boy said as he pulled Barney into a small cave to wait.

It was damp in the cave, and Barney's cramped position hurt his burns, but the boy had said to trust him, so he trusted him. In time, he slept while the boy watched and guarded.

He shook Barney awake. "Come. It is time for us to leave."

"Wait," Barney said, touching the boy's arm. "Why are you helping me?"

The boy looked at him with his sad, dark eyes. "Denise Saravena was my friend," he said. "After my mother died, Denise brought us food until I was old enough to join the army."

"Who is Denise?" Barney asked.

After a moment, the boy said, "Let us wash your wounds and drink at the waterfall. Then we must go. I know a small mountain village north of Puerta del Rey where we will be welcome."

They drank at the foot of the waterfall. Barney let the cold water run over his bare feet and stomach, washing away the putrefaction that had begun to develop in the burns.

It felt good. Barney's head began to clear. He tore his shirt to make a bandage for his hand so that he could hold the knife better. He tore off strips of cloth to cover his feet. As he was splashing water over his head and neck, the boy whirled around, his knife poised for throwing.

Out of the forest ambled a chimpanzee, chattering and running in a zigzag. The boy sighed.

"You know what you're doing with that knife," Barney said, relieved.

The boy lay on his stomach to drink. "No man knows more than the jungle," he said. He waded into the water to wash. Then the shot came and sent the boy sprawling into the mud at the other side of the stream, a hole the size of a grapefruit in his back, his thin legs twitching for a moment before he lay still.

Barney saw the soldier before he had a chance to turn around, so by the time he turned, his knife was already spinning in the air and came to rest with a thwack in the soldier's chest. The chimpanzee at the other end of the stream screamed and scurried noisily into the jungle as Barney scrambled back into the cave. Moments later, when the other soldiers appeared, they followed the noise of the chimpanzee. And Barney was safe to look on the lifeless form of his friend, a boy young enough to have been his son.

He waited an hour, staring all the while at the dead boy who had saved his life. None of it made any sense to him any more. Strangers come and then they go, and some of them hurt you along the way and some help you. And some even die for you. But why, God, why him? Why not me? I don't remember half my life, and this boy didn't even get to live it. Why didn't you take me instead? he said to himself, as he dug a shallow grave for the boy with a rock beside the stream.

Then, without thinking, without caring, he wandered aimlessly into Puerta del Rey the next morning, stopping to spend a day and a night in a sleazy café that served him three bottles of tequila in exchange for his brass belt buckle.

And after the three bottles were empty, Barney felt good for the first time in all the life he could remember. He felt so good that he called a press conference in the middle of town to say that the CIA was bad. The CIA was in Hispania. The chief of police, somebody named Estomago, looked surprised to see him, although Barney didn't know the man from Adam. He didn't want to know anybody. The CIA was here. The CIA was bad. And who the hell cared?

# CHAPTER FOURTEEN

Smith placed two pieces of paper side by side. One was the front page of the New York *Daily News*. The headline read:

## NATIONWIDE MARCH ON
## WASHINGTON
### Millions of Blacks Protest Murder of Civil
### Rights Leader Calder Raisin

The other paper was an enlargement of a microfiche from the Women's Correctional Institution in Abbey's Way, Indiana:

Mr. George Barra, Warden
Women's Correctional Institution

Dear Mr. Barra:

This is to inform you that your inmate #76146, Pamela Andrews (armed robbery, 25–life), continues to serve out her sentence satisfactorily under Hispania's voluntary work program.

May I extend my congratulations to you for your participation in this program. By permitting your prisoner to serve her term by performing much needed work in our country, you not only save your taxpayers many dollars in prisoner upkeep, but take a great leap forward in progressive penal reform as well.

I shall continue to inform you about the well-being of your inmate who has been transferred to our program, and offer you my best wishes.

General Robar Estomago
Chief, National Security Patrol
Republic of Hispania

A stack of similar letters, all dated two years earlier, were piled on the side of Smith's desk. He looked down at the notes he had made while reading.

—All the prisoners sent to Hispania on Estomago's voluntary work program were women.

—All were orphans.

—All the letters to the prisons had been signed by Estomago.

—All the prisoners were serving maximum sentences.

—All were doing well, according to the letters. No deaths, not even accidental.

—But not one of the CIA agents stationed in Hispania with Barney Daniels had recalled seeing any white women working on the island.

He looked again at the newspaper.

Calder Raisin, an ineffective leader in life, was a martyr in death. Blacks everywhere were rallying. Riots in Washington were feared.

The autopsy report on Raisin showed that he died from multiple contusions of the head caused by a variety of weapons. Daniels had been sent out to kill Raisin, yet Raisin had been killed by more than one man.

Gloria Sweeney had been in Hispania with Barney. Gloria Sweeney was now in New York, and probably tied up with Estomago.

A bomb in an envelope manufactured in Hispania had been placed to kill Barney Daniels.

And the blacks were marching.

The CURE director wheeled in his chair and looked out through his windows of one-way glass at Long Island Sound. The pieces of the puzzle were coming together and the picture that was forming was chilling.

First, there had been the appointment by Hispania's President De Culo of the American-hating Estomago as his U.N. ambassador.

And then, there were growing signs of Hispania drawing closer and closer to the Soviet Union.

Then, there was the ship. A Russian military ship, carrying what might have been nuclear equipment, had simply vanished on its way to Cuba. One day, it had been sixty miles from Cuba's shore. The next day, high altitude spy flights and spies inside Castro's empire couldn't find the ship. It had never arrived.

The report had arrived on Smith's desk and at first, he was willing to think it accident at sea. The ship had sunk. But as the days had gone on and the Russians had not announced the accidental loss of the ship, he had begun to wonder. And then, three weeks later, agents in Europe reported that the ship was returning through the Baltic sea.

So, where had it been?

Was it possible that the ship had swerved from its expected course at the last minute and arrived in Hispania to unload a shipful of nuclear weapons supplies?

Smith drummed a pencil against the back of his left hand. Ordinarily, he would had have discounted such a scare prospect as nuclear arms in Hispania. But there were other things that made it difficult to discount.

In European capitals, agents were picking up tips and rumors—rumors about a strike against the United States now being possible.

Was it possible? Could Russia be planning a strike against the United States? A missile strike launched from Hispania?

Gloria Sweeney and Estomago had been behind the killing of Raisin. Therefore they were responsible for the hundreds of thousands of blacks marching on Washington, D.C., right now. Was that part of some plan, to try to create such chaos and confusion in Washington that the nation's defenses might somehow be slackened? And what was the map that Barney Daniels had been talking about?

The CURE director sighed. So many questions; so few answers.

He would just have to wait for Remo to come back with some answers.

It did not occur to Smith to worry that while he was waiting, plans might be moving along to blow up a piece of the United States. Waiting was the correct thing to do. Therefore he would wait. And he would tell no one because the burden of responsi-

157

bility was his and no one else's. So he put the problem out of his mind, turned back to his desk, and began to look through the month's vouchers for Folcroft Sanitarium.

He shook his head in annoyance. For the second straight month, the bill for bread had gone up and he was getting pretty sure that one of the kitchen workers was stealing some of those food supplies. Something would have to be done.

# CHAPTER FIFTEEN

The big mosque on 114th Street was closed. Two black-suited guards watched the entrance, which was chained and padlocked.

Whistling, Remo strolled over to the chain and snapped it as though it were a peppermint stick.

"Wuffo you doing that shit," one of the Peaches of Mecca said as Remo walked through the gates toward the mosque. "I mean halt, man. Halt in the name of the Afro-Muslim Brotherhood."

"No time, boys," Remo called over his shoulder. "Catch you later."

"You gonna catch us right now," the other Peach said, and the two of them executed a flying tackle at Remo's knees.

He caught them in mid-air. Using one of them as a club, he twirled the man high overhead and smacked him into his companion's midsection with a thud. Two pairs of dazed brown eyes shone, unfocused, beneath their sweat-glistening shaved heads.

"You one mean mother," one of them said. The other shook the fuzz out of his brain and staggered to his feet.

"In the name of Allah," he said as he pulled a blue-tinged knife out of his inside coat pocket, his eyes locked into Remo's.

Remo kicked. With one stroke the knife was lodged into the guard's throat, a stream of red trickling onto his white shirt collar and spreading. The man stiffened and trembled. His mouth opened and closed like a fish, but no sound came out.

He wobbled a few paces in a zigzag line toward Remo, then reeled and stumbled. His mouth formed half a word: "Mother . . ."

Remo blew, and the small gust of air sent the man careening downward with a crash. "That's the biz, sweetheart," he said.

"Holy shit," the other Peach gasped as Remo turned to face him. "Look, man, I ain't got no knife, see?" Shaking, he opened his jacket. "No knives, no zip guns, not even a pea shooter. Just a country boy up here visiting my aunt Minnie, yes suh." He backed away. "Me, I'm strictly for nonviolence. Amen. Free at last." He took off at a brisk trot, peering behind him to see if Remo was following.

He wasn't. He didn't have any time to lose. He paused at the heavy double doors leading to the interior of the mosque just long enough to be impressed with the precision of their construction. It was airtight in there, and the doors must have weighed a half ton apiece. Whoever designed these doors was building a fortress, and preparing for siege.

159

Using a thrust from the elbow, he wedged his hand into the hairline crack between the two doors. It was solid steel, more than two inches thick. Feeling with his fingertips, he located the locking mechanism and jammed three fingers into it, releasing the lock with a deep pop, like a small explosion occuring far underground. Then he pushed with his shoulder to dislodge the interior bolt.

Inside, the mosque was as cold and silent as a cave. He passed room after empty room as he strode silently down the vast network of hallways and stairways, his feet barely touching the gleaming polished floors. He tapped on one of the walls. Steel. In a corner of the building, he felt with the balls of his feet for the underlying structure beneath the tile flooring. Again steel.

At the base of a small white metal stairwell, he saw the only other people in the mosque: two black-suited young men, their faces expressionless, their heads shaved and gleaming blue-black under the dim lighting. They appraised Remo coolly, acknowledging his presence by no more than a cold glance from heavy-lidded eyes.

They moved toward him like two panthers, silent, deadly. They were the best of the lot, thought Remo as he watched them move. Obviously trained to stay with Gloria as her personal guard.

Without a word, one of them snaked toward Remo in a flying arc, legs tucked tightly to his chest. Remo stood still, waiting for the inevitable foot to come jutting out at his solar plexis. When it did, Remo caught the heel of the man's foot and swept it upward to lock the knee. Then, with the leg straight and locked, he pressed the foot with his palm in a small, potent move that dislocated the man's hip and sent him howling down the length of

160

the corridor as fast as a bowling ball, until he came to rest with a splat on the far wall.

The other man moved, never taking his eyes from Remo, his face registering nothing.

He was fast. As he prepared his blow—a shoulder spin designed for use with a weapon—Remo noticed the man had good balance. "Not bad," Remo said. "Shame to have to kill you just to get to that white kitty in there."

The man began the spin, as evenly weighted as a cat.

"Beautiful," Remo said, as he pulled a packet of matches from his pants pocket and tossed them to the floor. They slid precisely between the tiles on the floor and the man's shoe. It threw his balance totally, so that when he came out of the spin all his energy had spun into his feet to stay upright. The man twirled to a stop, momentarily drained. Remo stepped in close to the man.

"Hold it, sweetheart," Gloria called from the landing. She was dressed in a diaphanous white sari that only partly concealed her body, and she carried a revolver.

Remo stopped. "At your service," he said with a bow.

"That's better," she said, and squeezed the trigger.

As Remo saw the tension in her hand, the small muscles of her index finger beginning to contract over the trigger, he collared the remaining guard. In a motion too swift for the guard to resist or Gloria to see, he put the man's body between himself and the bullet, and before the guard could register surprise, he was dead and Remo was up the stairs, the gun crumbling to pieces in his hands.

161

"Get in," he said to Gloria, shoving her inside her apartment.

"What for? There's nobody else around," she said disgustedly. "You knew that."

"I want to see the map . . . Miss Sweeney."

"Map?" She laughed. "Sure. Help yourself." She threw out her arm in a Bette Davis gesture to indicate the map on the wall. "Have an eyeful, sugar."

It was an ordinary world map. A little old, maybe, Remo thought as he scanned its worn folds, but nothing special.

"Barney Daniels is alive and talking, I suppose," Gloria said, a look of resignation settling over her features and rendering them haggard as she slumped into an overstuffed white chair.

"That's right. His memory's back."

She lifted a weary eyebrow. "It was bound to happen. Care for a drink?" She cocked a frosty glass in his direction.

"No thanks."

"It's only mineral water. Here. Try some." She eased herself out of the chair and poured a tall tumbler for Remo at the bar.

The glass felt cold in his hand. The moisture on the outside of the glass wet his skin. "I guess water wouldn't hurt," he said.

Then he smelled it. It was faint, almost nonexistent, just a tinge. "Ethyl chloride," he said, bewildered. "And something else. Something common."

"Don't be silly. That's just plain old $H_2O$, straight from the hidden springs of New Yrok City. Now bottoms up." She drained her own glass in one nervous gulp.

"And what was that?" Remo asked.

"Gin. I'm tapering off water," she said with a smile.

162

Remo smiled, too. He held his glass toward her. "Go on. Have a taste."

"No, thanks."

"Come on," Remo said. "You only live once." He squeezed her jaw open and poured the liquid down her throat.

"Ethyl chloride and mesquite," Remo said. "Mesquite like in tequila. That's what you hooked Daniels on, wasn't it? The mesquite. First, you fudged up his brain with ethyl chloride, then hooked him on the mesquite. And he kept getting enough of it in his tequila to keep the chloride pumping in his tissues, keeping him under. Until he dried out in the clinic."

Gloria sputtered and coughed. Remo squeezed the junctions of her jaws harder. Her mouth popped open wider. "Let's try this all one more time," Remo said and poured the rest of the decanter into Gloria's mouth. "Let's see what's in *your* system."

The liquid bubbled over her teeth. It sprayed. It dribbled down her chin and plastered her gauze drape to her breasts.

Abruptly, the woman stopped struggling. As Remo watched, a wild, happy glint lit her eyes. He released her jaw and she winked and smiled at him. She seemed unaware of the spittle running down her face.

"It good," she said, clapping her hands together.

"The ethyl chloride's in you too," Remo said. "Is that why you're involved in this? They got you with drugs?"

"Just a little drinkie now and then," Gloria said.

"Want to talk now?" Remo asked.

"Rather play feelies," she said. She raised her breasts toward Remo.

"Where is everybody?"

Coyly, she waggled a finger at Remo. Her face was twisted in a leer that she must have thought was a smile. "No, no, never tell." She giggled, then said, "All the niggies gone. Niggies, niggies, niggies. All gone to Washington to get blown up."

"Who's going to blow them up?"

Her face lit up. "Me. Gloria. And Robar."

"Estomago?"

She nodded. "The one with the big hose." She rolled her eyes appreciatively.

"Why do you want to blow them up?" Remo asked.

"Not just them. Everybody. All in Washington."

"I thought you loved the Afro-Muslim Brotherhood," Remo said.

She blurted a raspberry. "A game. Niggies got me sent to jail. Robar got me out."

"What'd you do to go to jail?"

She bent her neck down, then peered up at Remo as if she were looking over a fence. "Shot me a niggie and they sent me to jail."

"Poor little thing," Remo said.

"Poor Gloria," she said. She sniffed eloquently. Suddenly a tear blossomed from the corner of her eye. "Gonna blow them up; gonna blow everybody up."

"How are you going to blow them up?"

Gloria giggled. "With bombs, silly. Robar's got bombs. Lots of bombs. Let's play ficky-fick. Too much talk."

"First talk," Remo said, "then ficky-fick. Are the bombs in Hispania?"

She nodded. "At the installation. The girls put them together. Built the camp too."

"What girls?"

"The girls Robar got from the prisons. Like me.

164

Only I didn't have to work at the camp 'cause I'm so pretty." She patted her platinum hair.

"When are you going to explode the bombs?"

"Maybe next week. Maybe never. Whenever the Russians say so."

"What's going to happen to Hispania?" Remo asked.

Gloria shrugged. "Who cares? Robar and me, we going away. El Presidente, he going to Switzerland. Who cares? We got lots of money and we get lots more when the Russians come into Hispania and take the island over."

"Where are the girls now?"

"All dead. We shot 'em. Bang. I like shooting."

"Then why didn't you shoot Barney Daniels?"

Her eyes opened wide. "Cause he got away and came to America. So we sent him a bomb, but he didn't blow up. And then we made him kill Calder Raisin so he would go to jail and rile up the niggies. But he didn't kill Calder Raisin. He can't do anything right."

"Just a deadbeat, I guess," Remo said.

"Good ficky-fick though," Gloria said.

Remo walked once around the room. "I only want to ask one more thing," he said. "What's so important about that map on the wall?"

"Dopey," she said, fluttering over to the map. "It's a bomb map." She pressed a tiny button on the desk below the map and an overhead track light came on, illuminating the map with an eerie green light.

As the light glowed stronger, lines on the map began to emerge. Blue lines. Red lines. Dotted lines. And a thick, wobbling stroke from a jungle border of Hispania to Washington, D.C.

"El Presidente had it coated, so that you can't see

the lines without this special light." She smiled. "He's so smart."

"A real whip," Remo said.

Gloria seated herself on the window sill. "You gonna stay and play with me?"

"No."

"Aw, c'mon," she teased, unfastening the top of her sari and letting the gauzy fabric unravel and flutter in the breeze outside the open window. "Nice jugs, huh?" she asked.

"Good enough for government work," Remo said.

She unravelled more of her sari, until a long stream of fabric floated in the wind like a white river. She stood up on the window sill and lifted her arms to her sides.

"Look, I'm a flag," she squealed, stretching out her arms to grasp the billowing sheath. "I'm an angel! I'm flying! Death to the niggies!" she shouted. "The angel of death is flying! Death to America! Ficky-fick forever."

Then her feet left the floor and she soared downward, down the sheer face of the building, her garment unwinding behind her in brilliant white streamers as she fell naked to the ground below.

Remo shook his head. "Freaking nutcase," he said. "Everybody in this deal is a nutcase."

# CHAPTER SIXTEEN

Barney Daniels sat up in bed, rubbing the sore spot where the intravenous feeding needle had been taken out.

"Just a couple more days, Mr. Daniels," said the black nurse. "Then you'll be out of here. Can't happen too soon, either. If some of our regulars found out we had a white man here, I don't know what'd happen." She smiled at him.

"No," said Barney, shaking himself to life. "Now."

"Now, now . . ." the nurse began.

"Just once," Barney said. "Now. I'm going. Get Doc."

"Doctor Jackson is busy at the—"

"Get him in here." Barney's voice reverberated through the small private room. "Otherwise I'll run out front and tell the whole neighborhood that you're treating white folks. You'll never live it down."

"Just you calm down," the nurse said. "I'll get the doctor."

Jackson was harried and tired looking and Barney realized he could not remember a time when Jackson hadn't been overworked, overtired and underappreciated.

167

"What is it now, you honkey pain in the ass?" Jackson said.

"Sit down, Doc."

"C'mon, I'm busy."

Barney sat up and cleared a space on his bed. "Talk to me for a minute. We both need it."

Doc Jackson sat, his knees creaking as he bent them.

"Bad one?" Barney asked.

Jackson nodded. "Bullet wound. Some asshole went on a toot and shot his girlfriend in the face. I thought I could save her." He closed his eyes, the lids weighted by decades of sleepless nights and lost causes.

"Ever hear from your wife?" Barney asked.

"Sure." His grim black face cracked into a semblance of a smile. "When she wants more money."

"Your kid?"

"Ivy League. Majoring in revolution, relevance and hate. I'm not one of her favorite people. What's this all about anyway?"

Barney shifted on the bed. "No reason. I've just been thinking. Wondering how things might have turned out, you know, if Denise—"

"Stop it. Now. All the what if's and what-might-have-beens in the world aren't going to bring her back, no matter how bad you want her."

"I remembered, Doc. I remembered everything." There was such pain on his friend's face that Jackson could not ease it. All he could do was to spend this moment with Barney and listen to him.

"I remembered when things used to be important. Ordinary things, just living. Every day when I'd wake up, I'd be glad that I made it through again. Do you remember?"

"Me?" Jackson thought. "I don't know. I guess

168

so. But everybody gets over being young. That's all it is. You get older, you see things differently. You expect less." He shrugged.

"Bullshit," Barney said. "There's not a day goes by that you —you personally, Robert Hanson Jackson—don't wonder what the hell you're doing here."

"Oh, really?" Jackson mocked. "What makes you think you know so much about me?"

"Because we're the same guy. You're black and ugly and I'm white and handsome, but except for that you couldn't tell us apart."

"You flatter yourself," Jackson said. "So what's next?"

"I'm going to Hispania. Tonight."

"No, you're not," Jackson bellowed. "You're not leaving this bed for two days."

"I'm leaving now," Barney said.

"No way," Jackson said.

"Doc, I'm a little weak and maybe I can't take you. Actually, I guess I never could. But I can sure as hell wait until your back is turned, then punch the face off that nurse of yours. I'm going."

Doc sighed. "It can't wait? You're in no shape for a trip."

"You heard me talking under the drugs," Barney said. "You know what happened to me—what happened to Denise. I've got to start collecting some due bills. I can't wait any more."

Doc stood up with a sigh. "All right, you crazy bastard. Leave. I won't try to stop you."

"I'll need a couple of things too," Barney said. He picked up a note pad from the nightstand next to his bed. He tore off the top sheet and handed it to Jackson.

"Rope? What the hell kind of supply item is that?"

169

"I just need it," Barney said. He smiled at Doc. "Want to go on an island vacation?"

Doc snorted, his nostrils flaring. "That floating patch of parrot shit? Hispania? Shove it, pal."

He went to the doorway and stood there for a moment.

"The trouble with you, Barney, is that you don't know that you're an old man. It's all over for you. For me. We've just got to find something to keep us busy, something that doesn't make us feel too much like thieves. Something that lets us sleep at night."

"Like you," Barney said. "The first black everything. And your wife left you and your kid hates you. That's really something to live for."

"Better than nothing," Jackson said. "We're not thirty years old anymore. Neither of us," he said. "Wise up, Barney. Vengeance is a young man's game."

"Vengeance is mine, saith the Lord," Barney recited. He smiled at Doc, who hit the side of the door with the heel of his hand.

"I'll have your goddam supplies where you want them," Doc said.

Barney hurt.

He hurt walking out of the clinic, his clothes baggy and outsized on his now-bony frame. He hurt getting into the taxi that Doc Jackson had called and was waiting out front. He hurt as he stood across the street from the gates of the Hispanian Embassy, preparing his mind for what he must do. The thumb of his right hand pressed reassuringly against the steel handle of the scalpel he had filched from an instrument tray in Doc Jackson's clinic.

Barney breathed. He concentrated. He waited.

And then Denise came to him again, a shadow in

170

a lifetime of shadows. She spoke to him deep within the recesses of his mind.

"You have come back to me, my husband," she said, "I am proud of you this day."

And then Barney didn't hurt any more.

He walked across the street, toward the guard who was standing outside the locked gates, his rifle at port arms across his chest.

The guard stepped in front of him at the gate and pushed at Barney with the stock of the rifle. Barney's hand was out of his pocket, scalpel tightly in his fingers, and slashing across the man's throat.

Before the man hit the ground, Barney had the gate key from his pocket and let himself into the embassy grounds.

Another guard inside the front door tried to stop Barney. He reached out his hands to grab the lapels of Barney's jacket.

As he grabbed, Barney's hands moved up between his and caught the man's throat. Without his even thinking, Barney's well-practiced fingers moved into the right position, his thumbs pressing hard inward on the Adam's apple. He felt the man's hands loosen and Barney kept up the pressure until he heard a cracking sound, then a gurgle, and the man slumped slowly to the floor.

Daniels looked down at the body. How did he feel about having killed again? He looked at his hands. He smiled.

He felt good and he was just getting started. There were a lot of bills to be paid.

He removed the gun from the hip holster of the guard and walked down the long hall. At the end was Estomago's office, the door closed. Barney placed the heel of his foot near the lock and kicked hard. The door flew open.

Estomago sat alone at his mahogany desk. When he saw Barney, his face showed, first, surprise. Then terror.

"It's been a long time coming, you piece of garbage," Barney said in gutter Spanish.

"Wha . . ."

"You have a bill to pay for the death of my honored wife, Denise Saravena. And for the boy you killed for his help to me. I have come to execute you and send you to hell."

Estomago lunged for his desk drawer, for the warm reassuring magnum that he kept in there. But he was too slow and too late.

Before he could put his hand around the gun, Barney was leaning across the desk, the barrel of the .38 police special pressed into Estomago's forehead, directly between his eyes.

"It is not going to be that easy," Barney said. With his other hand, he slapped the desk drawer shut, then he yanked Estomago roughly to his feet and shoved him toward the door.

"Where are you taking me?" Estomago squeaked, his eyes round and glassy with fright.

"To the park," Barney said. "We finish as we began. With the ritual of the bat."

The telephone rang in Smith's office. He brushed an imperceptible moustache of moisture from his upper lip as he picked up the instrument.

Remo said, "Listen, this is all some kind of bullshit about nuclear weapons in Hispania being aimed at the U.S."

"Who is behind it?" Smith asked.

"Estomago," Remo said.

"Find Estomago," Smith said coldly. "Find out if

172

an attack is planned. If so, when. And then remove Estomago."

"Got it," Remo said. "You know something?"

"What?" asked Smith.

"This whole deal is all screwy as a can of worms," Remo said, "twisting and turning. I don't really understand it all."

"You don't have to," Smith said. "It's enough that I do."

"Gloria admitted that Daniels had been drugged by them in Hispania."

"Oh," Smith said. "What else did she say?"

"She said she could fly," Remo said.

"Could she?"

"No," Remo said as he hung up.


When Remo and Chiun reached the Hispanian embassy, a row of ambulances was lined up in front of the building.

Remo flashed a state department card and asked a police officer: "What's going on?"

"Don't know. Whole staff is dead or injured. Estomago's secretary is screaming some shit about a madman who tore in and took the ambassador, hollering something about a bat in the park."

Remo turned to Chiun and shrugged his shoulders. Making sure no one else could hear, Chiun whispered to Remo: "It is the ritual of the bat. A way of dueling practiced by many of the Spanish tongue. Daniels is no common killer."

"Daniels is in Doc Jackson's clinic," Remo said.

"Not any longer," Chiun said. "We will go to whatever park is nearest. When you find this Estomucko person, you will find Daniels."

\* \* \*

The clearing in the wooded area near one of the smaller ponds in Central Park bore a resemblance to the Hispanian camp from which the young boy had helped Barney escape. It was nearly the same size. The shape of the clearing was identical. It was all back in Barney's head now, all the memories, the murders, the tortures, the jungle, the young bride who had gone out to buy her man coffee and never came back.

And Estomago, this savage, who had killed her and Barney's unborn child.

Doc Jackson waited for Daniels and Estomago in the clearing, the bag of supplies on the ground beside him.

"You've been followed," Jackson said, as Barney shoved Estomago into the dirt. "His goons are right behind you."

"I know," Daniels said. "Tie us up and then clear out. They won't fire with him in the way."

"We can use him as a shield and get out of here," Jackson said.

"I'm staying," Barney said. "Get out that rope."

Jackson bound the wrists of the two men together with the length of rope. He blindfolded Estomago, then Barney, and placed a long knife in each of their hands.

"Leave now, Doc," Barney said. "Use us for cover."

Doc didn't answer.

"Don't try any heroics. Just get out. And Doc."

"What, fool?"

"Thanks for saving my life. I needed it for this."

Barney began to stalk Estomago in a slow circle around the clearing, listening for his footfalls and frightened breathing.

"You will not live through this," Estomago shouted, his voice trembling. "My men have instructions to follow me wherever I go. Half the Hispanian embassy is waiting nearby to slay you."

"You will not live through this," Estomago

The slash of a blade sang past Estomago's ear. He would not let the sound of his voice betray him again.

The two men circled. And Barney Daniels in his baggy clothes, his belly aching for food, heard once again the slippery animal noises of the jungle, smelled the lush tropical greenery. He was back outside the hut, fighting again for his life. Only this time he was not drugged, and he was not fighting a boy who had saved him from dying of thirst, and the crowd of spectators was not cheering.

This time he had to win.

Estomago stepped and thrust like a fencer, then jumped back and slashed around him. Barney heard the knife cutting through the air. He attacked from the other side, but Estomago was ready. He whirled out of the way with the grace of a bullfighter.

Robar Estomago had grown up fighting with knives. Despite his fear, he knew that the American was not accustomed to the blind fighting used in the ritual of the bat.

And Daniels was sickly. The past year, the constant abuse, the continuous consumption of tequila to satisfy the drug craving in his body, had all done their work.

Estomago breathed easier. He moved quickly on the balls of his feet, his poise returning.

Barney swung at him with the knife but the attack was slow and Estomago dodged easily.

"You have made a mistake," he hissed. "You know nothing of the ritual. I will kill you like a fly

175

on the wall." With that, he lunged forward with a low thrust. It caught the edge of Barney's left side. Estomago ripped outward.

Barney suppressed a scream and only grunted with the pain.

Doc turned to see Remo and Chiun standing alongside him, watching the battle. Across the clearing stood eight men, Hispanians, also watching.

"I can't help, can I?" Remo asked Chiun.

"No. It would be a dishonor to Daniels to be aided. We must wait," said Chiun.

Doc Jackson shook his head. Softly, he said, "He can't win. He's too weak. Too sick."

Chiun touched the big black man on the shoulder. "You forget," he said, "that there are such things as character and cause. He fights now for something besides alcohol poisons. Watch. He fights like the man he once must have been."

Across the clearing, Remo could hear the breathing of men waiting, their sweat sour with anticipation. He looked at Daniels, blood flowing from the wound beneath his ribs.

"Come, drunkard," Estomago said, a smile on his lips. "Permit me to kill you quickly before you bleed to death. It is more respectable, although why a whore's husband would care about respectability, I would not know."

He laughed as he parried again. His knife nicked Barney's shoulder. The rope tightened as Barney recoiled from the second blow. Estomago moved in quickly, preparing to slit Barney's stomach agape with one long slash.

He missed. As Barney ducked and rolled, coating the grass with his blood, he yanked on the rope and sent Estomago sprawling to the ground.

"Pig," the ambassador spat, bringing himself

176

slowly to his feet. "Now I kill you. For myself and for El Presidente." He threw himself at Daniels.

He held the knife overhead, then slammed it down toward Daniels's face. At the last moment, Barney turned his head and the knife slid alongside his cheek, burying itself into the ground.

Estomago reached behind him to remove the blindfold.

As he did, Barney's right hand reached over and his knife cut cleanly across Estomago's throat. The ambassador's last vision was of a wounded specter of a man watching him with hate-filled eyes, his blindfold pressed to the cut in his arm, standing in front of a pulsing fountain of bubbling blood. He heard Daniels say: "For Denise."

The knife dropped from Estomago's hand as he began to choke on his own blood, spurting with each heartbeat and staining the ground dark. His eyes rolled back in his head as he withered to the earth. Then, one quick convulsion, and the general lay still, the gash in his throat smiling upward like a giant red mouth.

And then the men came from across the clearing, armed with knives, stripped ceremonially for jungle fighting.

With a wave of the knife, Barney slashed the rope, freeing his wrist from Estomago's. Then he went into a crouch, holding the knife in front of him in his right hand. His left hand gestured toward the Hispanians, taunting them, urging them to come on, to join battle with him.

Remo looked at the gray-haired man in his dirty bloodstained clothes and knew this was someone he had never seen before. The Barney Daniels he had known had been a worthless drunk, done, washed out, finished with life.

But this man standing alone in the clearing was something more than that. Faced with death, he throbbed with life. He grinned as he waited for the eight killers.

And then he was not alone. To his right stood Doc Jackson. On his left stood Remo and Chiun.

"I don't need any help from you. From any of you," Barney snarled over his shoulder at Remo.

"Anything I hate, it's a surly civil servant," Remo said. Before he could say more, the eight men were on them, and the dozen men were turned into a human anthill, squirming with wild activity. Next to him, Remo saw Barney take down two of the Hispanians with straight-ahead knife thrusts that parted their bellies like a comb. One Hispanian soared out of the anthill like a rocket, flying free and screaming until he hit the trunk of a tree. He had found Chiun.

Another attacker leaped at Remo with his hands trying to close on Remo's throat. Remo rolled backward and put the man up and over. Just before the man's back hit the ground, Remo reached back and wrapped his arm around the man's throat. The man's back went down, but his head and neck stayed up, across Remo's upper arm and shoulder. There was a satisfying snap as the spinal column splintered.

Remo rolled up to his feet. To his right, he saw Doc Jackson struggling beneath the weight of a man with a blue-tinged dagger aimed at his eye.

He leaped forward toward the man, but before he could reach him, Barney Daniels whirled past him. With the side of his right hand, he swung at the temple of the man astride Doc Jackson. The hand hit with a loud clap, almost thunderous, and the man

178

dropped the knife, and slowly keeled over on his side, his skull shattered by Barney's killing stroke.

"Good work," Remo said.

They stood side by side and turned around. Jackson scrambled to his feet. The three saw the last two Hispanians advancing on Chiun.

"Shouldn't we help?" Daniels said.

Remo shook his head. "Don't worry about it." He called out. "Chiun. Be sure to keep your elbow straight."

Chiun did, straight through one Hispanian face, straight through the back of the skull, straight into the next Hispanian face, and then the two men's bodies were lying at his feet.

"Fair, Little Father," Remo said. "Just fair." He turned to look at Daniels, but Doc Jackson was already kneeling alongside him, checking the wound in his side.

"You are the luckiest son of a bitch in the world," Jackson said. "Another inch and bingo."

"I've got to be lucky," Daniels said. "I've got work to do." Then he looked at Remo.

"You know what's going on?" he asked.

Remo nodded. "The whole thing. Russian bombs. Threats to America. The works."

"Are you here now to kill me?" Daniels asked. When he said that, Jackson got quickly up to his feet, standing alongside Daniels, facing Remo.

"Naaah," Remo said. "I don't know any more. First it was kill you. Then it was don't kill you. I don't know anymore. I don't care. The next thing they tell me to do with you, they're going to have to do it by registered mail, return receipt requested. You're more trouble than you're worth."

"He always was," Doc Jackson said.

Barney looked at Remo and the eyes were clear and bright. "I know you don't want to tell me who you're working for," he said. "That's all right. But tell me this. Can you give me some time?"

"For what?"

"To finish my business in Hispania," Barney said.

"How much time you need?"

"Twenty-four hours," Barney said. He looked hard into Remo's eyes. "Please," he said. "I need this one."

Remo searched Daniels's eyes. He felt Chiun's soft hand touch his back.

Remo nodded. "For the next twenty-four hours, I think I'm going to be busy," he said.

"With what?" asked Jackson.

"Teaching Chiun to keep his elbow straight," Remo said with a smile.

"Thank you," Barney said. He turned to Jackson. "You didn't have to fight, Doc," he said.

The black nostrils flared. "I don't have to go to Hispania with you either, but I'm going."

"That makes you as big a fool as I am."

"No," Jackson said. "Just another guy who's tired of wasting his time and wants to do something good for a change."

"We've got two things to do," Barney said. "The installation and El Presidente."

"We're not getting them done here," Jackson said.

He turned away. Daniels looked at Chiun. "Thank you. Thank you both. This is something that's got to be done. Our government won't be able to get rid of that installation. Not with those lightweights in Washington. But it's got to go. You know that."

Remo nodded. "Let us know if you need help."

"Thank you. But we won't."

"No," Remo said slowly. "I don't think you will."

He nodded at Daniels who turned and put his arm around Doc Jackson's shoulders. At the edge of the clearing, the two old soldiers, off to chase their biggest, most frightening windmill, turned around for one last look at the thin young white man and the aged Oriental smiling benignly in his flowing robes.

Barney waved. Chiun nodded, then saluted them both.

# CHAPTER SEVENTEEN

"It's about time," Smith said. "Where have you been? It's been twenty-four hours. Have you seen the papers? Do you know what's been going on?"

"Which question should I answer first?" Remo said.

"What has happened?" Smith said. "You might try that one."

"I think everything has been taken care of," Remo said.

"Oh, you do, do you? Well, let me tell you . . ." but the telephone had clicked off and Dr. Harold W. Smith listened to a dial tone for four seconds. It took him those four seconds to realize that he had not slept in seventy-two hours and had not eaten in thirty-six. He had not seen his wife for three days. He had not played golf in five-and-a-half months. He had not taken a vacation in ten years.

After the four seconds were up, Smith pursed his lips in his lemon face and stood up gravely from the desk.

"Remo," he muttered, then swung the chair out of the way. He walked across the room, opened a cabinet and swung his golf bag over his shoulder.

As he walked out of his office, he glanced back and saw the *New York Times* folded neatly on his desk, the small bulletin in the corner of page one circled in red Magic Marker. For a moment, he thought of taking the clipping with him, then shrugged and walked out the door. All was well that ended well.

PUERTA DEL REY, Hispania (API)—A massive explosion rocked the southwestern corner of this island today. U.S. government sources said the explosion occurred in a secret Soviet military installation, and Washington instantly sent U.S. Marines to the site.

Whether the secret installation contained Soviet nuclear warheads could not immediately be determinded, because of the widespread destruction of the explosion. But, in a ghastly corollary, a mass grave was found near the installation where more than two hundred female bodies—apparently workers on the project—were buried.

El Presidente Cara De Culo, in the final development in this macabre series of events, was found dead in his palace only hours after word of the explosion at the secret installation.

De Culo's right hand had been cut off, and his body was found impaled on a large jungle knife. Whether the president took his own life by throwing himself on his knife was not known, but there were reports from government insiders that two men, one white and one black, were seen leaving the governmental

182

palace minutes before the president's body was found.

Who they were is not known, but already the streets of this small capital city are beginning to ring with tales of the exploits of "the demons of the north."

## FREE POSTER OFFER!

This full-color, 16 by 20 inch limited edition poster, reprinted from an original painting by Hector Garrido, can be yours—absolutely free—by simply sending your name and address, plus $2 to help defray the cost of postage and handling, to:

PINNACLE BOOKS
Destroyer Poster
1430 Broadway
New York, NY 10018

Act now—quantity is limited!
Offer expires December 31, 1981.
Please allow 8 weeks for delivery. Offer void where prohibited by law.